Rush

PALM SOUTH UNIVERSITY 1

KANDI STEINER

Published by Kandi Steiner
Edited by Betsy Kash
Cover Design by Kandi Steiner
Formatting by Elaine York/Allusion Graphics,
LLC/Publishing & Book Formatting

Episode 1

WELCOME TO PALM SOUTH

Cassie

PALM SOUTH UNIVERSITY. A small, private college tucked away in a shady haven right near the beach just south of Miami. When Mom and I took the tour around campus, I knew without a doubt this is where I wanted to be. The longboarding opportunities alone made me giddy, and the Bio-Med program sealed the deal. But now, standing next to my high school best friend staring up at a large house with Greek letters that mean absolutely nothing to me, I'm wondering if this was the right choice.

This campus is crawling with walking, talking Barbies.

"Are you sure we should do this?" I ask Paris, twirling a strand of my fiery red hair around my finger as she runs a small brush through hers. It isn't even noon yet and we've already been getting curious looks from the other new members in our breakout group. Redheads are like unicorns, and seeing two of them attached at the hip like Paris and I are is always a mystical sight to anyone who's not us. We've spent the past four years in high school trying to convince people that no, we aren't sisters, and I had a feeling we'd be having that same conversation here. At this point, it might be easier to just nod and go along with it.

"Um, duh," Paris says, rolling her eyes. "Why else did we come to college if not to live it up in a sorority? Hello," she draws out the word and starts counting on her fingers. "Parties, boys, lavish events, boys, study groups, boys. Need I say more?" She pulls her long red locks over one shoulder, showing off her delicate collar bone. She's always been extravagant, which aligns with her name perfectly. Her parents must have known what they were doing when they named their baby girl after the most fashion-savvy city in the world. Even now while most of the girls are in shorts and nice shirts trying to beat the Florida heat, she's in a designer sun dress that's only knee-length but I know is heavy enough to make her sweat. Yet somehow, she's not.

I laugh at her comment, but shift uneasily. I was excited to rush, but judging by the girls we've met so far, I'm not sure the sorority life is for me. We've already visited the Zeta Pi Alphas and Delta Beta Gammas. To be honest, I can't really recall anything specific about either because they were so much alike that they're blurred together in my brain. Both of them were stocked with beautiful blondes and brunettes with exactly the same body build and no interest whatsoever in anything that doesn't involve booze or boys. And don't get me wrong – I like both – but college is more than just parties and dates to me. I'm going to be a doctor, and this is where my journey starts.

I open my mouth to voice my uncertainty, but before I have the chance I'm cut off by our group leader clapping her hands together.

"Okay!" she squeaks, her rosy cheeks and big green eyes bouncing along with the dark chocolate curls in her hair. "Kappa Kappa Beta is almost ready for us. After this, we'll take a lunch break and meet up with the other new members before visiting the last two houses this afternoon. Any questions so far?" Silence. "Are you enjoying Spirit Day?!" Cheers. From everyone but me, that is. I just tuck my hair behind my ear.

Just as the screams die down, a cheer erupts from inside the house. All the potential new members, sans me, cheer back. After a few rounds of the cheering back and forth, a tall, long-legged girl steps outside. She's beautiful – smooth, creamy skin and exotic features, almost like she stepped out of a tequila ad. Her smile reveals perfect teeth as she clasps her hands in front of her hips.

"Good afternoon, ladies," she says, her voice polished and polite. "My name is Siomara and I'm the president of KKB. I know you've already been to two other houses today and you're probably feeling pretty overwhelmed." Some girls nod and Siomara smiles in return. "I hope you can relax a bit with us before lunch and just enjoy the conversation. Each of you is different. I know some of you will end up running home to other houses on this block, but some of you will soon be my sister. Regardless of which side of the coin you land on, I'm looking forward to getting to know you. And," she adds, smiling wider. "I have forty-two other sisters who feel the same."

Siomara steps to the side as the double doors open and reveal a group of equally beautiful girls dressed in various shades of teal and orange, Palm South's school colors. Every girl is smiling, cheering, and clapping along with an upbeat pop song as we walk through the doors. A perky blonde steps up to me as I enter, smiling as she laces her arm around mine and leads me through the house to a room that I assume is normally a family room. There's a large flat screen TV on the wall opposite a beige leather sectional and photos hung up all around the room. They're all of sisters in various settings ranging from community events to the beach. The first thing I notice is that the girls in the photos all look different from one another – a stark contrast to the girls in the other houses we've been to this morning. It's refreshing, and I feel myself relax a bit as the bouncy blonde guides me to have a seat at one end of the sectional.

"Hi," she says loudly, trying to speak over the rest of the noise as she takes the seat next to me. With their forty-two sisters and the twenty-seven girls in my potential new member group shoved in one house trying to speak to each other, it's a little loud, to say the least. "My name's Erin Xander." She holds out her hand and I take it in mine, shaking it firmly but not too hard.

"Cassie McBee."

"Pretty name!" She smiles wider. She has a classic face – rounded, but with well-defined cheek bones. Her large mocha eyes shine and I feel like I've known her forever even though we just met. "Welcome to the KKB house. How has your morning been so far?"

Erin seems friendly, but I know any minute now the shoe will drop and she'll start talking my ear off about things that probably don't matter to me. "Not too bad, I guess."

She frowns a little. "Well, hopefully by the time you leave here you'll have a different answer to that question." She crosses her legs, leaning in. "So, tell me a little about yourself, Cassie."

Wow. This is the first girl who's asked about me instead of just rambling on about how great her sorority is. "Well," I cross my legs to mimic hers. "I'm from Phoenix, I just moved here two days ago with my best friend, Paris." I point to Paris across the room.

Erin follows my finger and then turns back, smile still in place. "Awesome! It must be so fun rushing with your best friend."

"Yeah," I nod. "It really is. Although, she's a lot better at this than I am."

Erin cocks her head a little. "What do you mean by that?"

"I don't know, she's just more into the sorority stuff than I am, I guess. All the girls have loved her so far."

"Well," Erin says, leaning back a little. "It may just be that you two are growing up a little already, and maybe not in the same direction. Would you be okay if you ended up in a different sorority than she does?"

That thought makes my stomach lurch. "I don't know. We moved here together, we're rooming together , we're best friends – it only makes sense that we'd be in the same sorority."

Erin nods. "Yeah, it might make sense now, but don't let her make this decision for you. It's true what they say, you know." She pauses. "You end up where you belong. So, follow your heart and don't worry about what Paris is doing. If she's your best friend now, she'll still be your best friend after rush week – no matter where you end up." She smiles and I return the gesture, hoping like hell that she's right. "So anyway, what's your major?"

I cringe. "Um, Biology. I want to go pre-med."

Her eyes grow wide and I wait for it, I wait for the loss of interest, the *"Oh no, she's not here to party? That simply won't do."*

"That is amazing!" I blanch, but her smile remains intact. "I'm hoping to go to law school

11

when I finish here at Palm South. We can be study buddies together!" She giggles and I can't help but join her, the shock dissipating. "Oh!" she claps her hands together. "You have to meet my two best friends. You'll love them. Come on."

Erin grabs my hand and pulls me through the house, weaving between groups of girls until we reach a large kitchen, complete with granite countertops that remind me of home.

"Jess! Lei!" Erin drops my hand as we reach two other beautiful blondes. Uh oh, here we go. Here comes the we-all-look-alike-and-like-the-same-things. "Meet Cassie. She just moved here from Arizona and she's a Bio major."

"I'm Ashlei," one of them says, reaching her hand out for mine. She's slightly shorter than Erin and Jess, but I can tell just from the dress she's wearing that she must be really into fitness. Her legs are toned, her arms cut – she's gorgeous, but I can tell she works hard for it. "My grandma lives in Arizona. I love it there! Looks like you won't have to worry about giving up the weather. It's hot here, too." She winks.

"Yeah, but no one told me about this humidity." I point to my hair, which was frizzing out before I even left the apartment this morning. I'm sure it's a complete mess by now.

Jess extends her hand to me next. "Girl, that's one of the biggest problems living in Florida. Don't worry, we all go through it." She grins, running her fingers through her long, pin-straight blonde hair. Hers is a little darker than Ashlei's and Erin's is the darkest, but they're all blonde bombshells. I can imagine them turning heads when they go out in public together. "So what are your hobbies, Cassie?"

Again, not one of them has told me anything about the sorority. It sounds odd, but I actually love it. It's nice to know they're interested in me as a person, not just in selling themselves. "I'm really into school," I offer kind of sheepishly. "As nerdy as that sounds. And I longboard, so I'm looking forward to coasting around this campus."

"I just started longboarding!" Jess yells excitedly. "You'll have to help me when classes start. I'm a complete mess, but I really liked it."

"Yeah, it's not as easy as it looks, but it's definitely not as bad as skateboarding. I'll help you!" The loud music starts playing again, signaling that our time in the house is up. Even though I know I could potentially be back tomorrow, I'm kind of disappointed it's over already.

"Oh!" Erin laces her arm through mine again. "Looks like it's that time. Let's head toward the front so you don't get in trouble for being in here too long." She winks and I wave to the other girls as we start for the door. Just before we reach the foyer, Siomara waves to us.

"Thanks for visiting us today!"

I wave in return and Erin leans in to yell over the music, "That's my Grand Big Sister. Basically, she's my Big's Big." She chuckles at my confused expression. "Don't worry, you'll catch on. Anyway, she's brilliant. I'll have to introduce you next time!"

I smile, hoping there will be a next time. After the day is over, the sororities select who they want to come back another day as do the potential new members. It's all a secret, how the selection process works, but I know there's a chance I could get my list of houses to visit tomorrow and Kappa Kappa Beta could not be on it. "I would love that."

Erin offers me one last smile and a slight wave as we reach the door and I file back out into the suffocating August heat. South Florida is beautiful, there's no denying that, but it. Is. Hot.

I shield my eyes and make my way back to Paris. I'm so excited to tell her about my conversation with Erin, but before I can open my mouth she rolls her eyes and cuts me short. "Thank God that's over," she mumbles. "Those girls were so boring.

And did you see their house? Not even half the size of the Zeta house. Yawn."

I frown, my mouth pulling to one side. Since when does Paris care about the size of a house? "I thought they were cool," I say softly. "Nice. Different."

"I guess," she says, sighing a little, like she's too bored to argue. "Anyway, I'm excited for the Tri Phis after lunch. They have a swimming pool!" She jumps excitedly and we fall in line behind the rest of the girls marching towards the cafeteria. As we walk, I can't help but think back to what Erin had said about us maybe ending up in different places at the end of this week. My heart aches at the thought and I wonder if I'll even have the strength to write down a different choice than Paris when the time comes.

She smiles over at me and nudges me playfully and I smile back. College is about change, my parents have always told me. My sister said the same thing when she gave me my graduation gift. It's about growing, finding who you are and who you're not. It's about daring to live differently than you ever have before.

I wonder if part of that means friendships change, too.

Bear

"PLEASE PROMISE ME you'll have beer available when this week is over," Skyler whines into the phone and I chuckle, dropping the Xbox controller and moving back through the Omega Chi Beta house toward my room. It's the week before classes start, but already the house is filling up with brothers. It's loud as fuck and no matter how clean our housekeeper kept it over summer, we've somehow already found a way to make it dirty and smelly in here.

"Well hi to you, too."

"I'm serious," she says, but laughs a little this time. "I need alcohol. And also to not wear high heels for like, a year."

I close my bedroom door and fall back on the small bed, staring up at the ceiling. "You know we always have a rager on Bid Day. Too much freshman tail to pass up that opportunity."

"If I were there, I'd smack you."

"Whatever. You know your sisters do the same when we have rush week in the spring."

"Can't argue that," she says, sighing in defeat.

"How was the rest of your summer?"

"Busy. I had a tournament practically every week. It's weird," she adds, pausing. "People are starting to notice me. Like, they know who I am when I enter tournaments and stuff."

I lift my brows. "Yeah? That's awesome, Sky." Skyler Thorne is a sophomore, a year younger than me, but she's one of my best friends. We met last year on the annual Kappa Kappa Beta and Omega Chi Beta spring break trip and I recognized her from a poker tournament I watched on TV a few weeks before that. She was shocked that I realized who she was, but I follow poker pretty closely. Well, I follow *all* sports pretty closely. We started hanging out more and more after break and over summer until I went home to visit before the school year started. My face hardens at the thought of home, but I shake it off and focus on Skyler. "You know it's only going to get worse. You're too good not to get noticed, Sky. You're a winner. Winners don't get to stay in the background for long."

"Yeah, well, if I ever get that good, I'll have to enter tournaments with bigger prizes. I had to work all summer to pay for this year and I still couldn't give as much to my family as I wanted to. But I'm not ready for the big tournaments yet."

"Why do you say that? You know you could

win them. You're skilled, Skyler. You know your shit."

"I'm not that good, Bear." She sighs. "I still have a lot to learn before I belly up to play with the big boys."

I shake my head. "Whatever you say. You know I'm in your corner when you do decide to go pro."

"I know, and you know I love ya for it." I hear a loud voice yell in the background and Skyler huffs. "Gotta go, practice time. Apparently we aren't cheering loud enough."

I bark out a loud laugh. "Good luck with that. I'm going to go drink a beer."

"Hate you."

"Love you, too."

I go to end the call, but just as I'm about to push the large red button, my Mom's face pops up on the screen. I frown, but click the button to end the call with Skyler and answer hers.

"Hey, Mom."

"Clinton Pennington, why haven't you answered my phone calls? I've called at least ten times since you left last Saturday!"

I groan inwardly at the use of my full name. No one at Palm South has called me Clinton since my freshman year. I gained the nickname Bear after flag football season due to my tall, fit build and aggressive technique – in other words, I tackled people a lot. Skyler always says I'm more like a teddy bear, but that's really only with her. I don't show my soft side to many people.

"Because I'm busy. Why? You all out of drug money? Need me to break into my savings and send you more?"

"Don't get smart with me, young man. I'll drive down there and slap your black ass so hard my grandkids will feel it."

I sigh. "What do you want, Mom?"

"I wanted to check in and see how my son was doing, but apparently there's a crime against that in your book."

"I'm fine. Class starts next week. How are you?" I say the words flatly, not hiding the lack of respect I have for her. I know I shouldn't talk to her the way that I do – or at least, if she were a normal mother, I shouldn't – but she never earned the respect she demanded from me. And I'm finally getting to the point where I'm tired of giving it for no reason. I love the woman, I do – but I have no respect for someone who uses and abuses everyone in their life the way she does.

"Well that's good, sweetie," she says, her voice softening. "I miss you. Wish you would have just stayed up here for school." She pauses, waiting for me to say something but I don't. "Anyway, your brother is bringing the kids out this weekend. I'm sure he'll want to call and talk to you."

"Can't wait."

She huffs, but doesn't press me on it. My older brother and I are far from close and she knows it. The only person in that whole family who I genuinely care about is Clayton, my baby brother. He's only twelve, but already he's being exposed to the things I had to fight to get away from in Pittsburgh. He's the only reason I even visit during breaks. I'm the only positive role model he has, and I have every intention of reminding him what he can accomplish if he gets out of that house.

"Well I guess I'll talk to you then. Have a good night, Clinton."

"You too."

I end the call and toss my phone to the other end of the bed, letting out a long exhale. I don't have the chance to think about my fucked up family long before I hear my brothers yelling for me from the living room. I smile, leaving my phone and heading back toward the group.

I fall down in a large bean bag as my Little, Josh, hands me a cold Bud Light. I pop the top and throw it back, letting the sting of the ice cold liquid burn away the phone call with my mom. Looking around, I can't help but feel excited about the new school year. I'm a junior now and our fraternity is the top on campus. We're going to have a fucking blast this semester and I'm anxious to get started.

Thank God I have my fraternity brothers.

Real families are a disappointment.

Jess

I KNOW SIOMARA will have my ass if she finds out I snuck out to go to a bar tonight, but I'll take my chances. I'm going stir crazy being stuck in that house with all forty-one of my sisters. I love them, don't get me wrong, but damn – a girl needs a break.

And a penis.

Just saying.

I'm all about sisterhood and I truly do care about the new girls coming into our organization this year, but tomorrow is a late day – we don't have to be at the sorority house until eleven – so tonight, I'm getting drunk.

And hopefully laid.

I pull into a small beach bar and check my makeup once more before strolling inside. It's casual, not too many people, but it's a slightly older crowd which is exactly what I want. Fraternity boys are immature and stupid and I'm over their shit. I've spent the last two years wrapped up in their drama and I know that other than fulfilling my desire to not want to masturbate, they're not good for much. This bar is crawling with men in their mid to upper twenties – dress shirts, ties hanging loose around their necks – they're looking for a good time and I'm about to deliver them one on a silver platter.

My phone pings with another warning text from my Big Sister, Stacy. I sigh and type out a quick *don't worry, Mom* text to her before tucking my phone away again. Stacy and I are really close, but she graduated early last spring. Even though she continues to Mom me even after she graduated, she's still a bad ass mentor and one of the closest friends I have. I just wish I could say the same about my Little.

But that's a worry for another time.

Sauntering up to the bar, I take a seat on a bar stool facing the majority of the bar and scope out the possibilities. The bar is half inside, half outside and the breeze rolling in from the beach blows my long blonde hair out of my face, allowing me full view of the prospects. Just as I'm zeroing in on a group of guys at the pool table, the bartender strolls up to me and throws a small white towel over his shoulder, placing both hands on the bar in front of me before leaning over a bit. "What's your poison tonight, princess?"

I wrinkle my nose and pull my attention from the pool table to stare up at the man the voice came from. Instantly, the wrinkles leave and I swallow.

Holy hell, this guy is hot. And he's bald? I have never in my life found a man without hair even slightly attractive. I guess there's a first time for everything, right? My eyes fall slowly down his body, lingering on the muscles in his chest stretching against the dark red fabric of his work t-shirt. His tan skin is covered in tattoos, though I can't quite make them out in the dim lighting of the bar. My lips part slightly as my eyes drift back up to his face. He cocks a brow in amusement and I swallow again, sitting up straighter.

"Really? *What's your poison?* Could you be any more cliché?"

His other brow shoots up to join the first and his head cocks back, as if my words smacked him across that beautiful, chiseled jaw of his. "Wow. My bad. Is *what can I get you* any better?"

"Same thing, pretty much. But, regardless of how predictably you ask me, I'm still going to want the tallest glass you have filled to the top with a fruity rum and juice. You figure out the rest. Just make it strong."

He smirks, pushing off the bar and reaching down for a large glass. "Well okay then. You on vacation?"

"I wish. But, I can still drink like I'm on vacation,

right?" I give him a wink and he smiles, shaking his head a bit.

"I'm Jarrett." He slides me my drink and I tilt it to him in a *cheers* before taking the first sip. It's strong. And delicious.

Score.

"Jess. And this is scrumptious."

He chuckles. "Glad I could brew up your poison, princess." I glare at him, but he just winks and walks to the other end of the bar.

After I finish my first drink and order another, I wander up to the group of guys at the pool table. We play for a little over an hour, drawing an even larger crowd because – clearly – we're the most fun this joint has seen in a while. I'm cozied up and working on one of the hottest guys in the group when he informs me he has a fiancé.

Wow.

Buzz Killington, ladies and gentlemen.

I hang out with the group a little longer, hoping to move on to a new prospect, but they all head out before I have a chance to seal the deal with any of Mr. I'm-Engaged-But-You-Don't-Need-To-Know-That-Until-It's-Clear-You-Expect-To-Sleep-With-Me's friends. Sighing, I take my place in the same barstool as before and Jarrett slides a fifth drink my way.

I hold up my hands. "I should probably say no this time. It's almost closing time and I need to drive."

"Not necessarily," he offers. I eye him curiously and the corner of his mouth pulls up mischievously. He finishes wiping down a glass and hangs it above his head before leaning across the bar, his minty breath tickling my drunken senses. "You've been trying all night to get with that douchebag when I could have told you from the beginning that he wasn't available. And now, you're left with an ache between your legs that you don't want to take care of on your own. So yes, you could drive home, get up and go to work tomorrow and just try again another night. Or," he pauses, licking his bottom lip and dragging his teeth across the top as his eyes fall to my mouth. "You could give me your keys, jump in my truck, and let me take you back to my place so I can cure you of your current situation."

Oh hell to the fucking yes.

Keeping my eyes locked on his, I fish my keys from my purse and drop them on the counter, cocking a brow. Jarrett bites his lip as he grabs the keys and shoves them in his pocket.

"Give me five."

Four and a half minutes later, we're tangled up in the back seat of his truck. I run my hands down his incredibly cut abdomen and lift his shirt up and over his head as he pulls the straps of my dress down over my shoulders. His lips are hard on mine and his hands run the length of my body until they grip my hips so hard I'm not sure if I should cry out in pain or pleasure.

"Are you sure you don't want to go back to my place?" he pants, kissing down my neck. My eyes roll back and a moan escapes my lips.

"I think I'd rather see how all that talk holds up in the back of a truck."

Jarrett growls against my neck before biting down and lifting me from his lap. It's then I realize he's wearing dark gray board shorts. He quickly unties them and pulls them to his knees, followed by his boxers. And there he is in all his thick, perfect glory. I bite my lip and stare up into his dark eyes. They're hooded with desire and I feel the want spread through my entire body as he grips my hips again and lifts me up from the seat, rotating me to face away from him. His rough hands slide my dress up and over my thighs and ass, exposing me to the heat radiating from his body behind mine. There's a rip of a condom wrapper and seconds later, Jarrett leans flush against me and grips my hair in one hand, pulling my head back so he can whisper in my ear.

"Is this what you want, Jess?" He thrusts against me and I feel his hard cock against the curve of my ass. I inhale deep, need coursing through every vein.

"Yes," I breathe, biting my lip in ecstasy.

"Then take it," he hisses into my ear, running his tongue up my neck before sucking my lobe in his mouth. The feel of him against me combined with his breath hot in my ear evokes a loud moan from my throat. "Take my cock inside you."

He pulls my hair harder and I groan, maneuvering my body until I feel him at my entrance. Slowly, I push back against him and feel as every inch of him sinks deep inside me. I don't even try to be quiet anymore. Loud moans and screams rip through me as he moves his other hand up to grip my hair, too, pulling it back each time he pounds into me. He fills me over and over, our hot breath steaming up the windows in his Ford truck.

I push my hand against the back passenger window and it slips down, leaving my fingerprints marked on the glass. "Harder," I moan and Jarrett delivers, hammering into me with more force before smacking my ass. It stings, but I can't deny that I love it. I've never been spanked before, but now I'm tempted to beg for it again.

"Oh," I cry out and he runs his hands back up into my hair before trailing them down my back and over my ass. He holds me firmly in his grip before rearing back and smacking my skin again, this time with enough force to send me spiraling over the edge of desire. I climax hard, maybe harder than I ever have before and Jarrett quickens his pace before driving into me with slow, hard precision. I ride out my orgasm like a California wave, completely spent by the time it crashes on the shore.

But Jarrett isn't done.

Quickly, he flips me over to straddle him. My legs are Jell-O, I have no idea how I'm going to ride him after what he just did to me, but he pulls my legs up to prop my feet on the seat and then leans my back against the console, lifting his hips to meet mine. In this position he feels even bigger than before and he hits places I never even knew existed.

Jarrett slowly drags the palm of his hand through my hair and then over my face, the pad of his thumb catching my bottom lip before he trails it down my neck, my chest, my abdomen, and rests it between my hips. His thumb finds my clit and he begins a torturous circle against the already tender spot. I arch my back in response and he groans, plowing into me with the same rhythm.

"You didn't wait for me last time. That's fine. But you're going to come again. *With me*, this time." I moan as he pumps harder, his breath growing shallow. Just as his body starts to shake inside mine, I reach another climax and tremble with him, our bodies moving together in a sweet and passionate harmony as we cry out into the foggy air of the truck. Every touch is amplified and I feel every last thrust. When we finally slow to a stop, Jarrett remains inside me, the sweat from our efforts making our bodies stick together in every place our skin touches. I'm not complaining.

He pulls me forward slowly, my back aching from being pushed back against the console. Licking his lips, he brings my mouth to his and kisses me hard, branding me with a passion I've never experienced. And I don't care what time it is or how much sleep I lost by sneaking out to this hole in the wall beach bar tonight. I'd do it all again. This is the best sex I've had in a long, long time.

And I can't wait for round two.

Bear

I'M DRUNK. And it's hot as balls in South Florida. Therefore, I'm also sweating. But I don't give a shit because I'm drunk.

Almost all my brothers are back on campus now. It's the night before sorority Bid Day and we know we'll be raging all day and night tomorrow, but that didn't stop us from getting a head start tonight. My Little, Josh, is currently doing a keg stand that I know will land him on his ass but I can't help but hoot in encouragement.

"You better not let me down, Little Bro! I'll kick your ass!" I smack him hard on the back and he sputters a bit, but keeps going. Josh is kind of a douche. Okay, he's a really, *really* big douche. But I'm doing my best to mentor him into being a half-decent guy. I'll never understand his obsession with fake tanning, but no one can keep up with me in the gym like he can and I respect him for that. I wanted him to be my Little from the start of his rushing process last spring. A Little is someone you can bond with, but more importantly someone you can guide. Although, I'm not sure I'm much of a mentor.

Suddenly, I'm picked up on a few of my brothers' shoulders and carried to the other keg. I grab it with my hands just in time to avoid smacking my chin against the metal and my legs are lifted up into the air. Then the nozzle is in my mouth and I have a two second warning before the beer starts flowing.

Challenge accepted.

After forty-seven seconds counted out loud, I kick my feet a little and they drop me to the floor with a roar of approval. I almost spit out the last swig of beer when the room settles and I'm face to face with Skyler.

"Not bad, Bear." She grins. "Although I'm pretty sure you've done better."

I shake my head. "How the hell are you here right now? Tomorrow's Bid Day."

"What Siomara doesn't know won't hurt her. I figured I could trust you and your brothers to keep it quiet."

I frown, unsure if I trust them as much as she does. I scan the room for our president and drag Skyler with me when I finally find him. After whispering the situation in his ear, Matt whistles loud enough to quiet the entire house.

"Listen up!" he shouts above the music. "See this girl right here?" He gestures to Skyler and her face flushes a bit, but she stands straighter and gives a wink. Always so sassy, that one. "No, you don't. You don't see her at all. She isn't here. She never was. Got it?" There's a cheer of understanding and Matt nods once. "Carry on."

He smiles back at us and throws his arms around Skyler's shoulder. "There. Problem solved. If anyone finds out you were here, let me know and I'll haze the shit out of these fuckers. I don't care if they are brothers."

Skyler giggles a little. "Why thank you. And what do I have to do to pay off that favor?" She quirks a brow and tilts her head a little.

A sly grin creeps over Matt's face. "I can probably think of a few things."

"Alright," I throw my hands up and back away from them. "I'm leaving the two of you to settle your debts. Find me when you're ready for shots, Sky."

She gives me a wink and Matt's eyes scan the length of her toned body in the tiny shorts she's paired with a loose t-shirt. I know without a doubt that she dressed herself tonight. Usually, her sisters were dressing her up – *sororitizing* her or whatever. She's far from a dress and pearls type of girl. But tonight, in her natural form, I think she's prettier than she ever is when they doll her up in all that makeup and shit.

I get asked all the time if I'm into Skyler. Some of my brothers have steered clear of her even after I assure them we're just friends. For a while, I wondered if maybe there was something between us that we just weren't seeing – something we were giving off that made other people look at us the way they did. But, at the end of the day, Skyler is more like the baby sister I never had than anything else. I just care about her. And, surprisingly, she cares about me.

Plus, that girl can play some poker. And that is something I'll always respect.

"I'm sloshed." Josh grins and lifts the red plastic cup in his hand to his mouth once more. "What's up with Skyler being here?"

"She snuck out. Keep your mouth shut about it, Little. I mean it."

"I'm not saying anything," he says, his hands up in mock surrender. "She single?"

I nod toward her and Matt, who are now cozied up on the back couch, her legs in his lap and his fingers playing in her hair as they talk over their drinks. "Technically, yes. Not sure if that's going to matter much tonight, though. Matt moved in right after his little announcement."

Josh's shoulders deflate. "I want to bang her so fucking bad, dude."

I smack him hard across the back of his head and he curses, spilling some of his beer. "The fuck, man?"

"You know better than to talk about her like that around me. Show some fucking respect, douchebag, before I make you."

"Whatever," he mumbles, still rubbing his head as he stumbles off toward the beer pong tables. My phone vibrates in my pocket and I pull it out to yet another call from my older brother. Great.

He's been calling me all day, but until now I hadn't been drunk enough to answer. I almost always have to be intoxicated to deal with his shit. Who knows what kind of state he'll be in tonight.

"Hey," I answer simply, maneuvering through the house to find a semi-quiet spot. I settle on the back hallway that leads to the bathrooms.

"'Bout fucking time you answered your phone. What the hell are you doing?" His voice is high-pitched and springy and I know without even asking that he's high off pills.

Doubly great.

"I'm partying. Sounds like that makes two of us tonight."

There's a grunt on the other end. "You implying that I'm high, little bro?"

"Depends. Are you?"

He pauses, then sighs. "Listen, I didn't call to fight with you. I need your help."

Here we go.

"Let me guess, you need money?"

Another pause.

"The fuel pump went out on the car and I had to use the last of my check to pay for it to get fixed. I found a guy to do it for less than the shop was asking, but it still wasn't cheap. And now the boys don't have food." His voice trembles just a little when he says that last part, but I'm not sure if it's because of his high or the content he's spewing. "I just need a little bit, Clinton. A hundred bucks for gas and food. Please."

I curse under my breath and glance across the room where Skyler is watching me intently, her brows furrowed. "You can't keep doing this shit, Carleton."

"What shit? It's not my fault the fucking car went to shit." I wait for him to just admit the truth, but instead he grows more frustrated. "You know what? Whatever. My bad for thinking you would want to help your fucking nephews."

"Stop." I sigh, pinching the bridge of my nose. It's not even worth arguing with him over where his money really went. Regardless, his sons don't deserve to starve because of their father's piss poor decisions. "Give me twenty minutes to get to the store. I'll wire you what I can."

"Thank you, little brother. I love you. I'm so proud of you, you know."

I roll my eyes as he continues, his words falling on deaf ears. When I'm sending money, I'm a great little brother chasing my dreams in college. When I'm not sending money, I'm a stuck up brat who thinks I'm better than everyone else.

I startle a bit when Skyler's hand touches my arm. I lift my eyes to hers and when I see the worry in them, my face hardens. The last thing I need is anyone at Palm South knowing about my fucking family drama.

"Yeah. I'll call you with the confirmation number." I hang up before he has the chance to respond. Skyler is still staring at me, her hand gentle on my forearm. I think I'm shaking, but I can't tell.

"Bear, what's going on?"

For a moment I just stare at her. I blink. I breathe. Then I shrug her off and turn for my room.

"Nothing. I have to run an errand. Don't stay out too late, you know Siomara will throw a fit."

She chases after me. "Wait. What happened? Where are you going?"

I whip around too quickly to face her and her eyes grow wide. Sighing, I run a hand over my short, coarse hair and calm myself. "I just have to handle something, Sky. I'm fine, I promise. Just go back to Matt and have a good time tonight. I'll see you at the Bid Day Bash tomorrow. Cool?"

Skyler hesitates, chewing the inside of her cheek, but finally nods with a small smile. I try to return it, but it dies halfway and I turn back toward my room instead.

She doesn't follow this time.

Cassie

THE NIGHT AIR is still hot and sticky as I sit on one of the benches facing the campus fountain. I stare at the blank card in my hand with three lines that I've yet to fill. I'm supposed to pick my top three choices for the sorority I'll be in for the next four years of my life and hope that one of them chooses me back. Most of the girls in my small group filled theirs out right away.

Paris was one of them.

She told me last night that she was choosing Zeta Pi Alpha. "Suiciding" them is specifically how she put it, which means she only wrote them down on her sheet – not even allowing for a second or third option. If they don't choose her back, she won't have a home to run to tomorrow.

Which is kind of where I am right now. Without a home.

My group leader told me I could walk campus if I wanted to. To "clear my head". So here I am, staring at the way the light jumps off the water of the fountain each time it spews into the air and wishing it could somehow spout up the answer to what decision I should make.

There are a few houses that I actually like. Delta Beta Gamma has grown on me throughout the week and the Kappa Kappa Beta girls were super nice. But Paris went Zeta. And she expects me to do the same. Meanwhile I can't help but wonder if I should write down any of them at all.

"I love this pond at night."

I startle at the interruption of my thoughts just as a slender brunette plops down on the bench next to me. Her long, loosely curled hair falls over her shoulder slightly as she turns to me with wide blue eyes. They're slightly glazed, like she may be buzzed, but her smile is genuine and warm. "It's a great place to think."

I hold up the card in my hand slightly. "Well, I could use all the thinking power this pond can offer."

She glances at the card. "Ah, rushing a sorority?"

"At this point, I'm not sure."

"Well what are you thinking? Talk it out to a stranger. Might help." She smiles again and for reasons unknown to me, I feel like I can trust her. At the very least, I don't know her, which means she can't really judge me. And if she does, it doesn't really matter, I guess.

"I'm thinking that I'm not sure any of these places are for me. My best friend from high school is going Zeta but I know *for sure* that I don't fit in there. I'm worried about going somewhere else. We did this together. We were supposed to end up in the same house and have the next four years just like we had the last."

The girl thinks for a moment, her hair blowing in the breeze slightly. "Just because you don't rush the same sorority doesn't mean you can't still be great friends. You'll just have her plus your sisters. It doesn't have to be one or the other," she offers. "You said before you weren't sure any of the sororities were for you. You really think that?"

I sigh. "I don't know. There is one house that I really liked. All the girls seemed nice and actually interested in me as a person. But even still, I'm not sure I want to be Greek. I only did this because of my best friend."

She smirks, but pauses a second, as if she's looking for the right words. "You know, I felt the same way you did when I rushed." My eyes grow wide. I didn't think she was a sorority girl. "I came from a small town and, well, let's just say my life there was a lot different than I wanted it to be." She shrugs. "But here, I knew I could be anyone. On the last night of rush when I had to make my choice, a girl in the last house I visited told me that the best part of being in a sorority is always knowing you have a group of sisters who have your back no matter what. Through the good times and the bad, you've got someone there to fight through college with you. To me, that was the best thing someone could promise me." She nudges me lightly. "What about you? Do you want a group of friends who will be by your side for the next four years?"

I think about Paris and our group of friends back home. They were my sisters then, but already I can feel that bond breaking. Paris has changed so much just over the summer, I can't imagine what she'll be like over the next four years. I lift my head to meet the stranger girl's eyes and smile. "Yeah. Yeah, I really do."

"Well," she says, returning my smile and lifting herself from the bench. "Then think about who you've met this week and who you think would be great to have in your corner. I know you will fit in wherever you end up. And they'll be lucky to have you."

She turns to leave but I stop her. "Wait!" She's still smiling. "What sorority are you in?"

She laughs a little. "Well, I can't tell you, actually. That would be dirty rushing. But, just follow your heart. You'll end up where you belong." She adjusts her bag on her shoulder and my eyes fall to the embroidered letters on the side.

KKB.

I grin and look back up at her, but she never looks back as she retreats. And once again, it's just me, the fountain, and a decision waiting to be made.

But now, *finally*, I know how to make it.

THEY MAKE US sit on our bids in the gym for ten minutes before we can open them and find out what sorority we're running home to. Our group leader is trying to talk to us and distract us from the wait, but I feel like this card is burning a hole into my shorts right now.

I suicided Kappa Kappa Beta last night and I have no idea what's about to happen.

"Can you believe it? We're going to be *sisters*!" Paris squeals, squeezing my arm and bouncing a little. I smile back at her nervously and watch the clock on the far wall. Time has never passed so slow.

"Alright, ladies," our leader says after an eternity. "Open your bids!"

The gym fills with a combination of rustling and envelope tearing followed by screaming, laughing, and crying. I slowly, calmly rip the top of my envelope and stare at the card when I pull it free. And then, I exhale.

Kappa Kappa Beta.

"AH! OH MY GOD OH MY GOD I'M FREAKING OUT!" Paris grabs my card and suddenly her smile fades. "Oh no…"

I'm still smiling. "No it's okay, Paris. It's what I wanted."

She screws her face up. "What? What do you mean, *it's what you wanted*? We were supposed to both go Zeta, Cass."

"I know, but I just don't fit in there, Paris. And that's okay. You do, and I know they're going to absolutely love you."

She shakes her head, but doesn't press me further. "Well, I'm sure you'll like KKB, I just really thought we were in this together." She hands my bid back. "I guess I'll see you at the dorm tonight?"

"Yeah, for sure." I pull her in for a hug, though she seems stiff. "I love you. Congratulations. We're sorority girls!"

That seems to bring back a little of her pep and she squeezes me tight before squealing again. "I know, right?!"

"Just wait a second, why is everyone

celebrating?" our group leader interjects. "You're not home yet, ladies. Now… RUN!"

Everything turns to chaos. There are bags being tossed and girls tripping over their own feet as they clamor toward the doors and out onto the main campus road. I wait a little, but make sure I'm not last as we run toward Greek row.

Paris veers off at the Zeta house, looking back at me one last time with a sad smile. I blow her a kiss and keep running. Kappa Kappa Beta is the last house on the street. When I finally reach it, I'm completely out of breath. There are fraternity boys everywhere handing me flowers and teddy bears and giving me kisses on the cheek. I scour the crowd trying to figure out what to do next and notice all the KKB sisters are holding anchor-shaped signs with names on them. One of them says mine in all capital letters.

Making my way through the crowd, I smile when I see the hand attached to the sign. It's the girl from last night. Her long hair is pulled up into a high pony with strands falling around her face and her makeup is immaculately done. She looks so different from last night, but her smile is still the same.

"Looks like that pond has a little magic in it, after all," she says.

"Looks like it."

"I'm Skyler," she offers her hand. "Skyler Thorne."

I reach out to shake her hand but she pulls me in for a gripping hug, instead. When we pull back, I say what I wanted to say last night but forgot. "Thank you."

She winks. "We're just getting started."

Skyler takes me around the yard and inside the house, introducing me to other sisters and new members. We take so many pictures my face feels numb from smiling by the time we finish, but it's fun. Everyone is so welcoming.

"Okay, it's time to drink. Let's hit the back yard!" Jess, one of the girls I met earlier this week, pops up beside Skyler, waggling her eyebrows.

"No arguments here. What do you say, Cassie?" Skyler asks.

And at first, I'm not sure what to say. This week has been all about figuring out where I belong. But now, the decision has been made and school doesn't start until Monday.

I think it's time to enjoy myself.

"Hell yeah!"

They both cheer and we make our way through the house and up to the rooms. Apparently they room together, because as soon as we walk into the large, two-bed room, they each cross to a different dresser and begin rummaging through it. Skyler tosses a skimpy bathing suit back to me.

"Here, I think this one should fit you. You can change in the bathroom right here." She points to an open door leading into a large, white-tiled bathroom and I can see another bedroom on through the opposite door. I duck in, change quickly, and meet them back in their room. They each have sundresses on, Skyler in a cute yellow maxi dress and Jess in a short red number with no straps.

Jess tosses me a cute lavender sundress and I pull it on over my suit. They both appraise me, smile, and then we head back downstairs and out to the back yard. When Jess swings the door open and gallivants off, I have a hard time closing my mouth.

The yard is covered with people – guys, girls – all in letters. There's a blow up slip-n-slide on one side of the yard and a pit full of bubbles in the other. A few people are already in their swim suits, either laying out in the yard or wandering around. More and more people join them as I stare.

"We kind of have to sneak the drinks," Skyler says, sliding me a flask and watching over my back for someone. Who, I'm not sure. "Technically we're not supposed to drink on KKB property."

"Really?" I take a swig from the flask and my face twists, but I stomach it. Rum.

She nods. "Yeah. The guys can drink all they want at the frat houses, but our council is pretty strict about not allowing sororities to drink in or around their houses. I guess it's unladylike or something." She shrugs, taking the flask from me and throwing it back. "Whatever. We have our ways." She grins just as someone bumps me from behind.

"Whoa!" I feel strong hands grip me around my middle and steady me. "Sorry about that." I turn to tell whoever it is that it's fine but when I come face to face with a lean, dark-haired guy with a heart-stopping smile, I forget how to speak. Or breathe. "You okay?"

I nod, which I'm surprised I can even remember how to do. He smiles wider, revealing perfect, blazing white teeth and one dimple on the left side of his beautiful face. His eyes are dark – almost as dark as his jet-black hair – and in nothing but floral-print board shorts and a white fraternity tank top, his lean muscles are on full display.

I swallow.

The guy's eyes move from me to Skyler and back again as he removes his hands. I feel a slight sting on my skin where he was touching me when he does. "I'm Adam Brooks, Alpha Sigma." He reaches his hand out to me first and I shake it numbly before he moves to Skyler. He eyes us both carefully, grin still intact.

"Skyler Thorne. And this is one of our new members, Cassie McBee."

"Nice to meet you both. Although we have a problem."

Skyler cocks a brow. "Oh?"

"Yeah. You see, you've got a flask. I've been here at least two minutes now and you have yet to offer me a drink."

Skyler giggles. "Why, whatever were we thinking, Cassie?"

I find my voice and try to keep up with the banter. "We're not being very ladylike, at all!" Taking the flask from Skyler, I hand it to Adam, shaking slightly and hoping he won't notice.

His grin intensifies and his eyes assess me, falling down my body slowly before meeting my eyes again. "I knew you two would be good hostesses." He tips the flask to us before downing back a shot. Then, he reaches behind him and grips his shirt just behind his neck, pulling it up and over his head. My eyes immediately fall to his chiseled abdomen and toned chest and my throat is dry again.

Holy hell.

"Are you a freshman, Cassie McBee?" he asks and again I can only nod in response. He chuckles, tossing me his shirt and tipping back the flask once more before handing it back to me. "Welcome to Palm South!"

He takes off running and dives headfirst down the inflatable slip-n-slide, leaving me holding fast to the cool metal of the flask and staring like an idiot. Slowly, I look over at Skyler, my mouth still wide. She laughs, shrugs, then pulls her sundress up and over her head, too.

"What he said." She grins and then takes off running in the same direction.

And I realize this is it. This is the first day of the next four years of my life. I'm here to get a degree, and that's more important to me than anything else. But at the same time, I'm here to have fun. And right now, standing in a yard full of shirtless fraternity boys and sisters who will be by my side through all the shit college will throw at me, I know without a doubt there will be no shortage of fun in my life.

This is Palm South. This is Kappa Kappa Beta. And I am *so* excited for both.

Episode 2

"YOU LOOK LIKE YOU COULD USE A DISTRACTION"

Jess

THE FIRST WEEK OF CLASS is my favorite. It's syllabus week, which means we only go over the hell we're about to endure instead of actually getting any of it assigned to us just yet. As I take a seat near the back of my last Wednesday class, Scope and Methods of Political Science, I chug down the rest of the iced coffee I picked up on the way over and sink down into the chair. I'm still hungover from post-rush weekend and I can't wait to get back to the sorority house. I need a freaking nap.

I'm one of the last ones in and less than a minute later, the professor claps her hands together. "Alright, let's get the logistics out of the way, shall we?" She's a middle-aged woman with dark brown hair and a smile too cheerful for me at the moment. She's dressed modestly in an all-navy dress suit and dark red lipstick covers her bird lips. Yep, definitely fits the part of a political science professor. "I'm Dr. Louise Maynard and hopefully you all already know that this is Scope and Methods. If you're here, I'm also safely assuming that you're Poli Sci majors. So, show of hands, how many of you are pre-law?"

I raise my hand along with a dozen others and we all look around the room at each other. If Erin were in this class, she would raise her hand, too. Of course, she already took this course last year when we were sophomores.

Show off.

"I see, I see," she appraises as our hands slowly fall back down. "Well great. As you know, this course is required for the major. Let's jump into what the semester will look like." She leans back against the desk and crosses her ankles, pulling the syllabus out from a notebook behind her. "My Graduate Assistant will be here soon to pass out your copies. Take notes until then."

She starts going over class policies and grading. I groan when she says attendance is required and worth ten percent of our grade. I hate classes that count attendance. I'm paying for this class. I should be able to decide if I want to attend or not. But whatever, I don't really have a say in it. My parents let me do whatever I want as long as I keep B's or better, so that's that. Looks like my Wednesday evenings will get off to a late start. This class is from 5:30 – 7:50p.m.

Dr. Maynard is just wrapping up the breakdown of test scores versus presentation scores when the large wooden doors open, causing her to pause. I'm still jotting down notes as she claps her hands together again. "Ah! There he is. Class, this is my GA. He'll be helping out throughout the semester with grading and tutoring along with various other tasks." I finish my notes and lift my eyes to the front. When I do, I drop my pencil along with my jaw. "Jarrett, would you like to introduce yourself to the class? Tell us a little about your graduate program and career goals?"

Jarrett, AKA the guy who had his hands weaved into my hair last week, is standing tall at the front of the room with Dr. Maynard. He's dressed in black slacks and a teal Palm South button up that accentuates his tan but covers the tattoos I know are lining his arms. Definitely a huge change from the boy in board shorts I jumped in the back of a pickup truck.

He casually runs a hand over his smooth head before tucking both hands in his pockets and appraising the room with a small grin and a glimmer in his dark eyes. "Hey everyone," he says, clearing his throat. *Is he nervous?* "I'm Jarrett Locke. I graduated with my undergrad from PSU last spring and decided to stick around for grad school. I have a particular interest in government relations for non-profits, so I hope to one day have a career where I can explore that passion daily." A few of the girls around me sigh and I fight against the urge to join them. Holy swoon. Please, someone wake me up. Someone tell me I don't want to bone my professor's graduate assistant.

Or that I already did.

"And I have nothing but faith that you will do just that," Dr. Maynard says, beaming at Jarrett. "Okay class, that's all for today. Jarrett's going to call attendance and then you're free to leave."

I repeatedly try to swallow as Jarrett goes down the list of names and one by one, students get up to leave. *Why did my German ancestors have to leave me with a name close to the end of the alphabet?*

"Jess Vonnegut," he says, my last name rolling off his lips slowly.

I stand and quickly throw my messenger bag over my shoulder. "Here," I chirp and bolt for the door. He checks me off and glances up quickly before his eyes fall back to the clipboard in his hand. When he realizes what he just saw, his eyes snap back up to mine.

Crap.

I cringe and try to duck away from his glare as I make my way up to the front of the room toward the door. It feels like it takes me ages to walk there, and his eyes never leave me. I feel them burning into my skin every step of the way. When I reach the front of the room and cross right in front of him, I chance meeting his gaze. And instantly regret it.

His eyes are smoldering, dark, hungry – and they automatically ignite the same animalistic fever he inflicted on me last week. I gulp and he closes his mouth, opens it again like he might say something, but then snaps it shut.

"Fuck," I mumble under my breath, pulling my eyes away and breaking through the door. I hold my breath until I reach the end of the hallway and burst out of the glass doors to the outside world. Panting, I pull out my phone and send a text to the girls.

- Emergency meeting. My room. Ten minutes. -

When I make it back to the sorority house, Erin, Ashlei, and Skyler are all waiting in mine and Skyler's room. "Oh my God," I say immediately, tossing my bag down on my bed. "You are never going to believe who the graduate assistant is in my Scope and Methods class."

"Oh! Are you taking Dr. Maynard?" Erin interjects. "I love her. Whoever her GA is, they're lucky. She's the best professor in the department."

"Yes, I am. And he may be lucky, Ex, but I'm definitely not."

Ashlei checks her phone for the second time since I've arrived. "Spill, Jess. You're not making sense."

"It's Jarrett." I wait, but they all just stare back at me so I sigh and toss my hands in the air. "The guy? From last week? Hot bartender, *super* hot truck?"

"Oh shit!" Skyler says at the same time Erin gasps, "No!" Ashlei just laughs. I toss a pillow and smack her square in the head with it.

"I'm sorry," she says through her laughter. "It's just, only you, Jess. Only you."

I groan, plopping my ass down on my bed and covering my face with my hands. "I know, right? Motherfucking fuck, dude. I really wanted to bang him again!" This time they all crack up and I toss pillows until I run out of ammo.

"Well, you win some you lose some, J-Love," Erin says, wiping a tear from the corner of her eye. I grin at the ironic use of my nickname. They gave that to me freshman year when I said I was "in love" with every single guy I dated. Luckily, heartbreak got me out of that phase. Now I just have fun with boys – and it's a lot less stressful that way.

"Shit," Ashlei murmurs, typing out a text on her phone before hopping off Skyler's bed. It's then that I realize she's got a gym bag packed and thrown over her shoulder. "I have to go. I'll see you later."

"Where are you going?" I ask, appraising the bag.

Her eyes dart around the room but she smiles confidently. "Just the gym. Then maybe out for a while."

"Hell yes, I could use a drink," I say. "Where you going? Ralph's?"

"Um." She hesitates, shifting. "I'm not sure yet. I'll text you after the gym. Love you!" Then she's gone.

Skyler and Erin eye me curiously. "Don't ask

me, she's been weird since we got back. Did either of you talk to her over the summer?"

"I called and spoke to her a few times and we chatted on Facebook," Erin says, taking her spot on Skyler's bed. "But other than that, not really."

"Yeah, I saw her during Shark Week but that's it," Skyler adds. Since we're the Palm South Sharks, there are always huge parties and events during Shark Week on campus. I was on a cruise with my family this past summer and missed it.

"Hm..." I kick off my wedges and fall back against the cool sheets of my bed. "I don't know, maybe I'm thinking too much into it. She's probably just busy with the first week of classes. What are you two doing tonight?"

Skyler looks at Erin and they both shrug. "I was going to see if Cassie wants to hang out, but other than that, no plans," Skyler says.

"Girly movie night? I've got a bottle of wine stashed under my bed." I waggle my eyebrows.

"Done and done. I'm already stressed from classes this semester," Erin says. "I'm going to change into yoga pants. Be right back!" She trots out of the room just as Skyler types out a text on her phone.

"I invited Cassie," she says, dropping her

phone to the bed. "I really think I want her as my Little, Jess. Do you like her?"

"Yeah, she's cool. But if you want her as your Little you better put in work. Jamie Dapreese has been hanging out with her a lot since Friday, too."

Her eyes widen. "Really?"

I nod, grabbing the remote to our TV off my bedside table and powering it on. "Yep. I saw them having lunch today between my two earlier classes."

"Well," Skyler replies, kicking back and letting her shoes fall to the floor, too. "I'm Skyler Fucking Thorne. I love Jamie, but she doesn't have shit on me. I'm going to show Cassie a kick ass time in the next few weeks and she'll realize our group is the best place to be in this sorority."

"Well, duh," Jess says, winking. "Just beware. You know Jamie, she likes to buy everything she wants – even if what she wants is a person and not an actual thing." Skyler nods and I know she's thinking back to Jamie's past boyfriends and all the shiny toys she's bought them. She's clever, that girl.

"Noted. Alright, what are we watching?"

"Something with lots of smut," I say, flipping through the channels. "I need a sexual distraction."

Skyler giggles and I smirk, still looking for something that fits that description.

When I find a channel with a Rom Com on, I drop the remote and grab the wine bottle from underneath my bed. After a few swigs, I start to relax. So what if the bartender I hooked up with is one of my teachers now? At least he's just the GA and not the actual professor. *That* would be awkward. Still, I was sort of hoping for a repeat of that magic he gave me in the truck. I had so many scenarios imagined already. The shower, the bed, a public dressing room, his kitchen…

Sighing, I take one last pull of the wine before passing it to Skyler. Oh well, no use dwelling on it now. He's off limits.

Right?

Skyler

I CAN STILL REMEMBER the first moment I knew I wanted Erin as my Big Sister. I met her during rush week and I knew she was smart, I knew she was driven, and I knew she wanted to do big things in the sorority. But that wasn't what won me over. It was two weeks after I rushed that I realized she would be the perfect Big for me.

We snuck a bottle of whiskey into her room in the sorority house and played truth or dare, just the two of us. By the time we finished half the bottle, we were drunk, crying, and had each been tasked with at least a dozen dares that made for a lot of great stories that semester. Seeing her let loose that night and opening up to her about my past was what sold me on wanting her as my mentor. She didn't pity me for the poor circumstances I came from or my loser high school days. Instead, she promised she'd help me reinvent myself at Palm South. She was the first one who told me I could convince anyone I wanted that I was the shit. And I believed her.

So far, it's paid off.

And now, I want to be that same choice for Cassie. She reminds me a little of myself when I was a freshman last year, except I'm pretty sure she was just as popular in high school as I know she'll be here. Me, on the other hand? I didn't have a single real friend in high school. My family was dirt poor. We played poker to pass our time. Little did I know then how much that would play into my future.

"So are you hanging out with her again tonight?" Ashlei asks. She ties her hair up into a high ponytail and starts packing up the rest of her stuff spread out on the bed. She's been listening to me worry over Cassie choosing me as her Big for the past hour.

"She's supposed to text me after her last class. I know Jamie already asked her to go to some fancy steak place for dinner tonight too, though, so I guess we'll see."

"You think she'll bail to hang out with you instead?"

"I don't know. She doesn't strike me as the kind of person to bail on anyone, but I guess I'm hoping she does."

Ashlei smiles. "You're so cute. She's going to pick you as her Big, Sky. I see the way she looks at you. She admires you already."

"I hope you're right, Lei. It's just…" I trail off. "Erin and I were always hanging out last year, but I can already tell she's going to be busier this semester. And then she wants to run for a position for next year. And then she wants president. When is she going to have time for us?"

"You know she'll make time," Ashlei says pointedly.

"I guess, but I still want an awesome Little to add to our family. Someone I can depend on, someone I want to hang out with. I haven't really connected with any of the other new members like I have with her."

"It'll work itself out," Ashlei says again, reassuring me. Suddenly, her door flies open and Jess and Erin waltz in.

"Dudes. We're drinking tonight," Jess says, pointing at each of us. "Put on your party panties and let's go."

"I can't," Ashlei says, zipping up her bag and throwing it over her shoulder. Standing next to Jess, their similar features are on prominent display. Long blonde hair, tan skin, lean figures with curves in all the right places. Ashlei is just a bit more toned than Jess, but their body types are almost identical. Where Ashlei has playful chocolate eyes, Jess has more of a hazel hue, but in low lighting they're pretty much the same. They're like twins. Except they're polar opposites.

"Where are you going now?" Jess asks, her hands outstretched toward the bag Ashlei just slung on. "Are you in some sort of gang we don't know about? A roller derby squad? A porn star league?"

"I'm meeting a friend at the gym and then we're supposed to work on a project together."

"A project? Already? It's the second week of school, Lei." Then her eyes grow wide. "Wait a second. Who's this *friend*? Oh my God, are you keeping a guy from us?!"

Ashlei blushes and looks a bit uncomfortable, but just shrugs in response. "We're juniors now, Jess. It's not all fluff in our classes anymore. I'm going to the gym and then working on this project. That's it, nothing more to tell."

Jess still seems skeptical, but she sighs in defeat. "True story. I already have a paper due for Scope and Methods next Wednesday."

"See?" Ashlei kisses Jess' cheek. "I'll see you at breakfast tomorrow." With that, she's gone and Jess turns to us.

"So, you two in?"

Erin declines and starts telling Jess about some sorority council sleepover she's going to so she can rub elbows with other sorority officers on campus just as my phone pings with a text. It's Cassie. She's going to dinner with Jamie. I sigh.

"Okay, you've got to come drink with me, Sky. You're the most fun anyway."

"Hey!" Erin says, smacking Jess playfully.

"What? You know it's true!" She grins, turning back to me. "What do you say?"

"Yeah, I'm in," I reply, sighing again.

"Speaking of fun," Erin says. "Omega Chi Beta is having their first social on September twenty-second. And," she pauses for effect. "It's an ABC theme! We're going, right?!"

ABC. Anything But Clothes. It's one of the most cherished social themes because the outfits are, well, endless. Anything but clothes, goes.

"Oh hell to the yes," Jess says without hesitating.

"Ugh," I groan. "I can't."

"What are you talking about? Why?"

"I have a poker tournament that night."

Erin and Jess exchange awkward glances. "Oh," Jess says. "Well, can't you just do a different one or something?"

"It doesn't work like that. I already paid the entry fee and it's the best payout they're having at the casino downtown for a while."

Erin's eyes soften and I know she knows. She's the only one who understands my parents' financial situation. "Are you sure you can't make it? Not even after the tournament?"

I shake my head. "It'll go all night."

"I don't understand why you play anyway," Jess says. Her words sting a little, but I try not to let them affect me. "It's a total boys' game." I don't respond and she sighs. "Sorry, but seriously, it is. Anyway, let's go drink."

"Actually, I think I'm going to pass," I say, standing from where I'd been sitting on Ashlei's bed. "I'll see you guys at breakfast."

Jess throws her hands in the air. "Are you serious? What does a girl have to do to find a drinking partner around here?"

Erin laughs and I give an apologetic smile as I slip through Ashlei's door and out into the hall. Pulling out my phone, I text Clinton.

- I'm coming over. Need to talk. –

He's been short with me since the party during rush week and I can't figure out why, but two seconds later he texts me back.

- I'm here. See you soon. –

I smile. Clinton and I met during Spring Break last year and he's the only one at PSU who got excited when he realized I play poker. I just wish he could transfer that excitement to my sisters.

When I get to the O Chi house and make my way back to his room, the music is already thumping through the house and brothers are lining up shots in the kitchen. Most of them look like they just woke up to start their days and it's already seven. Gotta love college.

"Your brothers are reckless," I say when I reach his room. He smiles, not even trying to argue. The Omega Chi boys are known for their partying. It's one of their best selling points during rush.

Clinton pats the spot on his bed next to him. "I taught them well. Come here." I sit down and he pulls me into his large chest. "Bear hugs fix everything."

I giggle before pulling back. "I can't argue that."

"What's going on?" he asks. He almost seems back to normal, but his eyes keep drifting to his phone on the bedside table and I know there's something going on that he isn't telling me. But, it's not my business to pry. I know Clinton. He'll tell me when he's ready.

"It's my sisters," I confess, sighing. "I can't go to our first social because I have a poker tournament, and they just don't understand. Erin still thinks I can just bail on them and Jess looks at me like a nasty bug on the ground every time I bring it up."

"What about Ashlei?"

"She hasn't been around much, but she's sort of in the same boat as Erin. I know they don't mean to hurt my feelings but… it just sucks. I want them to get that it's more than just a stupid hobby to me."

He leans back against his headboard, thinking. Clinton's room is one of the best in the house, design wise. He's got a thing for interior design, and I've never known another guy to keep his room as clean as Clinton does. It's themed in beiges, dark greens and mints with décor strategically placed to make the room appear bigger than it really is. His bedspread is a dark forest color that pulls out the slight hint of green in his hazel eyes. "You're right – I know for a fact they're not trying to hurt your feelings. But, Skyler, you have to understand their perspective, too. These are girls who were born into money – good money. They don't know what it's like to work for it yet. And poker? Please. Other than the blackjack we play at fundraisers, these girls are clueless when it comes to the game."

"So why don't they ask me more about it then? It's not like I couldn't teach them."

"Probably for the same reasons you don't ask them to show you how to do your makeup or how to shop for the dresses that will make you look skinnier or whatever. It's not their thing, Sky. And, to be honest, that's what makes you so special –

because it's not something you share with many other people."

I smile at that and chew on his words, digesting his point of view. "Yeah, I guess you're right." Thinking back to high school, my smile fades. "But... what if I don't want to stand out? What if I'd rather... blend."

"I think the key is finding a balance. You can fit in without becoming someone you're not."

"Such wise words, Bear," I joke, cocking a brow. Feeling more at ease about my situation, I turn the conversation to him. "So, you going to tell me what that phone call was about at the party last week?"

His jaw tenses. "It was nothing."

"Bear..."

"Don't," he says, jumping to his feet. He runs his hands through his short hair and inhales a deep breath before expelling it from his chest. "Sorry, I'm just not in the mood to talk about it. I'm fine, though."

I study his features, and without even a minute passing I know he's lying. Clinton's poker face is weak, at best. He wears his emotions on his sleeves, whether he wants to or not. But, again, I know he'll tell me when he's ready.

"Okay. I need a drink. Let's go take shots with your brothers."

He laughs, but his eyes still wear a coat of worry. "Yeah, enough of this girly talking shit. I need tequila."

With that, we make our way into the kitchen and join in on the drinking games. Slowly, all the stress I had when I walked through the door starts to fade. After my third shot, Matt, the Omega Chi Beta president, slides up behind me and starts nibbling on my earlobe.

"Come to my room," he whispers and tiny goose bumps flow from where his lips graze my skin all the way down to my toes. I follow him back and throw Clinton a devious smile on the way. He just shakes his head and chuckles.

"You look like you could use a distraction," Matt says when we reach his room, closing the door behind us.

"You have no idea." I slam my mouth on his and before long, poker is the last thing on my mind.

Bear

LAST NIGHT GOT OUT OF HAND. What started as just a few innocent drinking games with brothers turned into a rager that lasted until just before the sun came up this morning. It's just after three in the afternoon now, but I'm just finding the energy to pull myself out of bed.

When I sit up, I immediately regret it. A sharp pang shoots through my head and I squint against it, grabbing my phone off the bedside table.

No missed calls or texts.

Cursing, I unlock the screen and type out another text to Carleton. When I finish, it pops up into our conversation along with the seven other unanswered messages from me. Typical. I send him money and he disappears from the face of the earth. I can't stop thinking about my nephews. He knows I worry, which is exactly why he doesn't answer. It makes it easier for him to ask for money when he knows I care.

A girl's groan breaks the silence and I startle, whipping around to find another body in my bed. *The fuck? Was I really that drunk last night?* All I can see is one tan leg outstretched from beneath the covers. The rest of the body, including the head, is still buried beneath them.

"Well that was an interesting Tuesday night," Skyler mumbles, throwing the covers off.

"Why are you in my bed, Sky?"

"Come on," she remarks with a look that implies the answer is obvious. "You know I don't sex and sleep. I sex and leave. Only, I was too tired to do the second part of that mantra last night, so I settled for leaving his room. If it's under the same roof but not within the same walls, it doesn't count as sleeping with them, right?"

"You're ridiculous."

"You cuddled with me last night." I blanch and she barks out a laugh. "Kidding, Bear, kidding. You do snore though."

I grin, but slowly reach for my pillow and then tackle her, holding it playfully over her head while she squirms beneath me. I tickle her sides and she shrieks hysterically, kicking at me to no avail. Suddenly, my bedroom door flies open.

"Uh…" my Little trails off, standing at the door with wide eyes. "Should I come back later?"

Skyler is still giggling as she smooths out her hair and jumps up from the bed. She's in nothing but a tiny tank top and boy shorts, but she's not the least bit ashamed. She starts shimmying into her jeans like it's a normal everyday occurrence for us. "Hey Josh. He's all yours," she says, nodding toward me. "I was just on my way out. Class in twenty. See you!"

And with that, she pats Josh on the shoulder and happily skips out of the room. I smirk as Josh watches her walk all the way down the hall before turning back to me, eyes still wide. "Holy shit. Did you fuck Skyler Thorne?"

"Bro," I deadpan.

He throws his hands up. "I won't say a word, I swear. But come on, you *have* to give me details."

I roll my eyes, standing and pulling on my sweat pants. No wonder it looks like we slept together. We were both in our underwear. "She's like a sister to me, dude. Don't act like you don't know that."

"Yeah. A seriously hot sister you don't mind going incestual for." I punch him hard on the arm and he winces. "All right, all right, I get it. You didn't sleep together. You just *slept* together." He winks. "Your secret's safe with me."

"I give up."

"Hey," he says, changing the subject and following me down the hall to the kitchen. "Check this out." He shoves a small pink piece of paper into my hands and I squint to read the cursive writing beneath the bold letters: NOTICE.

"Is this a sound violation?"

"Yeah. Last night was epic," he answers with a goofy smile.

"We need to watch that shit," I say, crumpling up the notice and tossing it in the trash. I reach into the fridge for the orange juice with my name on it and chug it straight from the jug. "We're already on thin ice after Spring Break last year."

"Whatever. What are they going to do?"

"They could suspend us, Josh."

"Nah." He waves me off. "They won't. We're too fun. By the way, I'm throwing an unofficial social tonight. First one of the year. Stoplight theme."

"Seriously? Did you not just hand me a sound violation notice? Maybe we should lay low until the weekend." It pains me to say it, seeing as how a stoplight social is one of my favorites. You wear red if you're taken, yellow if it's complicated, and green if you're single. I always love hooking up with the chicks dressed in yellow. Those girls are working through some screwed up shit and they love having revenge sex. And me? Well, I'm the first one to volunteer.

"Bro, relax," he says, clapping me on the shoulder. "It'll be fine. See you later, I'm going to actually make an appearance in my chemistry class today."

I'm still glaring at him disapprovingly when he bounces out of the kitchen. He's *way* too energetic for me right now. Sighing, I place the OJ back in the fridge and resolve to let it go. He's right – we'll probably be fine. And, truthfully, anything to get my mind off home is welcome right now.

I guess I better clean up the yellow Jordans.

Jess

"WAIT, WHAT?" I ask my Little incredulously, standing from where I'd been sitting next to her on the couch in our sorority house living room. She cringes a little, but repeats what I thought I heard the first time.

"I don't want to take a Little."

I groan, pinching the bridge of my nose between my fingers. "What are you talking about? You've been in a year, it's time to take a Little. This is how it works, Bo." I look to my petite Little pleadingly, but she doesn't budge.

"I'm not ready, Jess. I thought I would be, but I'm not. I want to take a Little, just not right now. I need another year."

The front door swings open, letting in the fading rays of sunshine from the evening light as Ashlei walks through the frame.

"Oh thank God," I say. "Please, help me talk some sense into my Little, Lei. I'm at a loss for words."

Ashlei eyes us both hesitantly before dropping her gym bag to the floor. Her hair is high in a ponytail and she looks like she's been sweating. I really need to get on her level if I'm going to be taking pictures next to her this semester.

"What's going on?"

"Bo doesn't want to take a Little," I let out the words in one exasperated sigh. "I think it's her Asian-ness popping up out of nowhere."

Bo throws me a look, but her mouth actually curls up into a small smile. My Little is part Asian and she's absolutely gorgeous. We always joke in good spirit about her heritage, so she knows I'm not being mean when I say that. She pokes fun at my German heritage, too – especially when I try to get the first tan of the season and end up burning like a lobster, instead.

"Okay, well… if she doesn't want to take a Little, is that really the end of the world?"

My jaw drops. "Are you kidding me? It's an honor to get a Little and you know that! Sisters who don't get Littles are devastated until they finally do. And I know for a fact that there are at least two new members who want Bo as their Big."

"Is that true?" Ashlei asks Bo. She only nods in response. "Oh… well why don't you want to take one?"

Bo opens her mouth to answer but I cut her off. "There is no logical answer. She's been in a year, she's been a Little for a year, now it's her turn to be a Big."

"But that's just it," Bo says loudly, standing and tossing the pillow that was on her lap to the side. Her brows pull together and her long, sleek black hair slides behind her back as she stands. "I've been a Little, but I don't feel like I've had a Big."

My mouth snaps shut and I blink, not sure what to say. Ashlei shifts uncomfortably.

"I'm sorry, but it's true. You and Stacy are so close. I thought we would be the same way, especially after she graduated, but we've barely hung out since I became your Little. It's like you hung out with me nonstop to get me to choose you as my Big and then just stopped trying. I mean when is the last time we did something together just the two of us?"

I scoff and turn to Ashlei, looking for help. I don't find it.

"I can't argue with that one, Jess," Ashlei says apologetically. "Maybe she's got a point here."

"We hang out all the time!" I shout a little louder than I intend to. "We just hung out the other night."

"Yeah. At sisterhood movie night. But when is the last time we did something just the two of us? Something not sorority related?"

I chew my lip, but can't come up with an answer. She's right. I know she's right. Hell, I was just talking to the girls about how I wish I were closer with Bo. But right now, I don't want her to be right. I don't want this to be about us. I want her to take a damn Little and not let our family line die.

"Whatever." I snatch my Lilly Pulitzer bag off the couch and throw it over my shoulder. "Do what you want, Little. I'm late for class."

"Jess..." Ashlei tries to stop me, reaching out for my arm but I shrug her off and jet for the door, letting it slam behind me. I'm fuming. Bo should want to take a Little, she shouldn't be so fixated on what our relationship is like. I'm her mentor. That's what I'm supposed to be. Not every Big/Little pair is best friends. It's a special relationship, just like a big and little sister in real life. Yes, sometimes friendships bloom out of that sisterhood, and yes Stacy and I are an example of that. But, Bo shouldn't be holding back because she's searching for that with me, too.

I frown at myself as I speed walk into the Political Science building. *God, I'm being such a bitch.* Here my Little is basically saying she just wants to be better friends with me and I'm yelling at her telling her to go find new friends.

Yeah. I suck.

I snatch a packet of papers from someone as I storm in the classroom and up to a seat near the back. It's only when I sit down and unload my textbook that I realize I snatched those papers from Jarrett. He's watching me intently, his dark eyes narrowing as his brows pull in. I grit my teeth and start scribbling in my notepad as hard as I can with my black ink pen, trying to work out the tension that I know only has one true release.

A release I'd really like to get from my professor's assistant right now.

By the end of class, all the muscles in my body are growing sore and I know I can't take it any longer. I ignore Ashlei's text asking if I'm okay along with Jarrett's concerned glare asking pretty much the same thing and head straight to Ralph's after attendance is called and Dr. Maynard excuses us. What a fucking Wednesday.

Ralph's is a small, shitty bar but it's the closest one to campus and therefore always packed. It's something between a biker bar and a club and it's pretty much my home. As soon as I sink down into the barstool, I feel a little better.

"You need a drink," a deep voice says from behind me. I quickly glance back and fight the urge to roll my eyes. It's Matt, the president of Omega

Chi Beta. He's always been a huge flirt, which is kind of a lame turn-off to me, but I can't deny that he's hot. Bleach blonde hair, hazel eyes, cute grin and tall frame? Yeah. He'll do.

"I have one," I point out, lifting my fruity rum drink in his direction before taking a sip.

"Let me buy the next one?"

"I've never been one to turn down free booze." Eying him, I take another sip. "I'm surprised you and your brothers aren't throwing another rager tonight."

"Yeah well, we're trying to lay a little low after last week's stoplight party. Cops were called, tickets issued, alumni freaked out. You should have seen Bear ripping into Josh. I've never seen him so pissed off."

"Skyler said he's been acting weird lately."

Matt frowns. "Yeah, he kind of has. But I think it's just school shit. And his Little is a dick, so there's that."

I laugh. "Yeah, there's that."

Matt's eyes fall to my lips. "You have a beautiful laugh."

Rolling my eyes, I drain the rest of my drink and nod toward the perky bartender at the other side of the bar. She slides me a refill and I nod to Matt. "It's on his tab."

"Ruthless," he says, whistling.

"Hey, you offered."

"Indeed I did," he agrees. "But you were supposed to fall for my stupid pick-up lines."

"Do you want to have sex tonight?" I ask bluntly.

He chokes on his beer, wiping at the corner of his mouth quickly. "Um…"

"Let's cut to the chase here, Matt. You're a horn dog. You're buying me drinks. It's clear where you want this night to go, and luckily for you I've got some tension to work out and I'm more than happy to take it in that direction, too. So," I pause, slamming back the fresh drink he just bought me and licking the last of it from my lips. "Where to?"

He leans in quickly and presses his lips to mine, running his hand back through my hair and gripping it lightly. I'm a little bored, but I let him kiss me anyway and we make out like high schoolers until I feel him dragging me toward the door.

"Wait." I pull away from him, breathless. "My bag is behind the bar. One sec." I rush back to our bartender and she retrieves my bag from the back. When I sling it over my shoulder and turn back to find Matt, I find dark brown eyes, instead.

Jarrett is staring at me from the other side of the bar. His head is low, his elbows propped on the bar as he sips on a dark liquor. He swallows and his jaw tenses as his eyes flick to the door where Matt's waiting for me. I swallow, too, but lift my bag higher on my shoulder and make my way to Matt. He kisses my neck and runs his hands down my backside when I reach him, growling in my ear about what he can't wait to do to me.

As he tugs me out the door, I look back over my shoulder, expecting to see Jarrett still watching me. But he's gone. I frown, more disappointed than I care to admit, but force a smile when Matt pulls me the rest of the way through the door.

Matt's fun. I like the way he peppers me with kisses as we move between the sheets of his bed and I can't say I'm not surprised to see he's packing more than just a wallet in those frat shorts of his. But, I know I should feel guilty right now.

I should feel guilty because it's Matt's hands touching me, it's his mouth on mine, it's his cock driving into me, but it's not him who's responsible for my moans right now. It's not him that's making me scream as I orgasm in his bed.

No. It's Jarrett. Because all I can think of is him and those dark brown eyes.

And that mother fucking truck.

Skyler

I CAN'T STOP SMILING in the limo ride to Ralph's. Somehow, I landed Cassie as my Little. I've known all week – found out on Tuesday and have been showering her with gifts and clues ever since – but tonight was the night *she* found out, and it was priceless.

"Did you really not have a clue that it was me?"

"Well, I hoped it was, but all your clues threw me off!" she says, giggling. "You said you had blonde hair and you were a Poli Sci major. I thought it was Jess at one point."

"Well I wanted it to be a surprise!"

"It definitely was," she says, still smiling. Our limo is packed with ten other girls. It's tradition after Big/Little reveal that all KKB sisters convene at Ralph's, a dirty, old bar just off campus that's been around longer than the library. Most of the new Big/Little pairs take limos just for fun. It's cheesy and kind of lame, but it's tradition.

"Hey," I say, touching Cassie's shoulder when I notice her smile slip. "What's wrong?"

"Nothing," she tries, shaking her head. I give her a pointed look and she sighs. "I don't know. I'm so happy, Skyler. I am. I was freaking out thinking you weren't my Big but you are and now we're going out and it's going to be so much fun. But…"

"You're thinking about Paris, aren't you?"

Cassie frowns. "She's changed so much already, Skyler. She's always been a little… refined, I guess. But now she's getting snobby. And mean. And it's like now that we're not in the same sorority, she doesn't think it's fit for us to hang out. Like, ever. I don't understand it."

I really want to punch this Paris chick right in the left tit, but for now, I need to make Cassie feel better, so I put on my happy face. "Listen, she's just going through the growing pains. College changes people in a lot of ways. I know sisters who have plenty of friends outside of the sorority and friends in other sororities, too. If Paris is saying that's why she can't be friends with you, she's using it as an excuse for something she's been thinking for a while now."

Cassie's frown deepens and I realize that probably didn't make her feel better at all. *Cool. Great job, Skyler.*

"But do you remember what I said when we first met? By the fountain?" I ask and Cassie nods. "Well, it's still true. Your time in KKB is just beginning, but just know you've got an army of sisters on your side and we all want to get to know you better and form a lifelong friendship with you."

She smiles at that. "I know. I'm excited. And you're my Big!"

I squeeze her in a tight hug. "Hey." I pull back, assessing her. "Did I ever tell you the stories behind some of the girls' nicknames?" Cassie shakes her head no. "Well, I just realized we probably sound completely crazy to you, huh?"

She giggles. "Sometimes. It's kind of hard to follow."

"Well, let me clear it up. So, Ex is short for Erin Xander. Also, it's kind of an inside joke between the other girls and I that she's always someone's ex, never someone's girlfriend. We're still not sure how that happens." Cassie laughs and I join her a bit before continuing. "Lei's is easy, it's just the second half of her name. Everyone has always called her Ash and she bitches about it, so we call her Lei to get her to shut up."

Cassie chuckles again and I see the worry start to truly fade. "I like that. Kind of like how they call you Sky."

"Right," I agree. "It's just a shorter version of our names. J-Love's is the most fun, I think. It's kind of like J-Lo, but J-Love. It started because she used to say she was in love with every guy she hooked up with. Now, it's just because she's a heartbreaker. That girl is always hooking up with all kinds of hotties on campus and making them fall in love with her. Man eater, that one is." I smile, shaking my head. "I try to keep up with her and give her a run for her money, but it's tough."

"What does Bo stand for?"

"Oh, that's her actual name. It's Chinese for precious, I think."

"Neat." She pauses. "What do you think my nickname will be?"

I look up toward the neon ceiling of the limo, contemplating. "Well, you'll be Little Nug to me. That's all I really know right now. But who knows, maybe you'll get a nickname from the girls, too."

"I like Little Nug."

I smile just as the limo pulls to a stop in front of Ralph's. "Me too. Now let your new Big buy you a drink!"

"Um," she stammers, wrapping her fingers in her wild red hair. "I'm not twenty-one."

"Neither am I," I say with a wink. "Not yet. But, according to these…" I trail off, pulling two fake IDs from my purse. "I'm twenty-two and you just turned twenty-one last week. Happy birthday!"

We both laugh together as we file out of the limo and into Ralph's. The bouncer checks our IDs with a smirk and I'm pretty sure he knows they're fake, but he lets us in anyway and slaps neon green wristbands on our arms. Perks of being in a college town.

We meet up with Jess, Bo, Ashlei, and Erin at the bar. Jess is still a little sour about Bo not taking a Little, but she apologized to her earlier this week and they're trying to work on building their relationship before adding another sister to their line. I actually kind of think it's smart. Erin and I are pretty close, and Cassie seems like the perfect addition to the family. They haven't had much one-on-one time yet, but that's mostly because Erin is insanely busy. With the way Cassie is showing interest in school already, I have a feeling they'll have that in common, soon.

Jess and I exchange glances and devious smiles when Matt shows up with Clinton and a few more of their brothers. We found out earlier today that we're officially eskimo sisters – meaning we shacked up with the same guy. Although, luckily, neither of us have any hard feelings. He was a distraction for me and he figured that out when I showed up wearing green to their stoplight party. Jess feels the same way – though she did mention he may be distracting her again in the near future.

Adam Brooks slides up to the bar right between Cassie and I just as we finish our fifth game of flip cup. His dark eyes are hooded from his buzz and he grins goofily at each of us. "Well if it isn't the slip-n-slide sisters."

"Wow," I turn to face him completely, bringing my drink with me. "I like our reputation already, Little."

Adam's brows shoot up. "Little?" He looks from me to Cassie and back again. "Well hot damn. Congrats, ladies."

"I guess that means you should buy us a shot, right?" I ask as Cassie blushes and tucks her hair behind her ear. She's so innocent and cute. *Dear Lord, help her with being my Little.*

"You know what," he says, leaning up with a grin. "You are absolutely right."

He orders us three lemon drops and we throw them back and talk between more games of flip cup. My buzz is pretty strong now and the more I see his little dimple, the closer I lean in.

"You girls should come to the A-Sig concert next month."

I cock a brow. "Oh yeah? No offense, but Alpha Sigma events are usually pretty lame."

"Yeah well," he says, tilting his drink back. "I'm going to change all that this year." He throws a wink at Cassie and I can't help but smile. This kid is cute.

"What do you think, Little Nug? Should we go?"

Cassie's grin grows wider. "Well it wouldn't be a party without the slip-n-slide sisters, would it?"

Adam points two fingers in her direction. "She's got a point."

"I guess it's settled then. But, I do have one condition."

"Oh?" Adam asks, amused.

"Dance with me." I don't give him the chance to reply before I pull him out onto the packed dance floor, sticky with spilt liquor. Throwing my arms around his neck, I move my body against his in time with the heavy bass of the music.

After a few songs, I lean in and speak over the music. "So, you're changing Alpha Sigma's reputation, huh?"

"That's the plan. As long as my douchebag president stays out of the way."

I smile, my lips grazing his neck just a fraction. "Better be careful messing with the man in charge."

He shrugs, pulling back to catch my eyes with his. "What can I say? I like a challenge."

I return his grin and just like that, there's a new player at the table.

Bear

I WAKE TO A LOUD BANGING on the front door Sunday morning. I know it's loud because I never hear a knock from my bedroom but this one sounds like it's thumping on my head. Groaning, I swing my legs over the edge of my bed and make my way down the hall. Whoever it is continues to bang until I quickly pull the door open.

"About fucking time," the guy on the other end of the knock says, pushing past me into the living room. I bow up to him and he rolls his eyes. "I'm Alec. I was president of Omega Chi Beta six years ago and I'm here to save your ass."

"What the fuck did you just say to me?"

"Did I stutter?" he asks. *Dick.* "My name is Alec Carriker. Are you Matthew Dishman?"

I shake my head. "He's down the hall. What are you doing here?"

"I'd rather talk to Matt about that."

I cross my arms over my chest. "Well he's asleep and insanely hungover and I'm probably the only brother you're going to get a sober conversation out of right now. So if you don't want to wait around for several hours to get whatever has your panties in a wad off your chest, you can start talking now."

Alec steps up to me, his chest puffing out as his eyes level with mine. He's just as tall as I am, which I'm not really used to, but his frame is lean where mine is stout. "I don't know where you get off talking to an alumni that way, *boy*, but I'm about five seconds away from reminding you why you shouldn't."

"*Boy*?" My nose flares and I beg myself to calm down, but I'm not sure it's going to work.

He rolls his eyes. "Oh please, don't start with the race card. I didn't mean boy like that, I meant it as in you *are* a boy. You are young, you're naive, and you have no respect for your older brothers."

"I don't give my respect. You have to earn it. And you're doing a piss poor job right now."

Alec appraises me for a moment before exhaling a long breath. "Look, I didn't come here to fight. But, I'm pissed off and so are a lot of other alum. We got a call from nationals and they're assigning me and two other brothers to mentor the chapter for the rest of the year due to the copious amount of shit you've been getting yourself into."

I gulp, but don't respond. I know exactly what he's talking about. After last semester, the crazy parties over summer, and the now four times we've had the cops called on us this semester – it doesn't surprise me nationals has stepped in. But it worries me.

"So what does this mean?"

"It means you're in a pretty precarious situation and if you don't listen to me and get your shit together, you're going to get suspended. Or worse." He gives me a pointed look and my jaw tightens.

"I'll go wake Matt."

"Don't bother." He sighs, looking around the house. It's disgusting. Empty cups and beer bottles litter the tables and the floor and it smells like ass. He turns his nose up. "Just let him sleep, I'll come back later." He pauses. "I didn't catch your name."

"You didn't bother to ask. I guess *boy* will suffice for now."

He smirks. "Look, I'm sorry. I'm just... I'm really tied to this fraternity. I don't want to see it go down in flames. What's your name?"

I frown, but extend my hand anyway. "Clinton Pennington. Everyone calls me Bear."

"Bear," he tries my name and I know he's wondering why anyone would call me that. Or maybe he's figured part of it out by now. "Well, Bear, I'm sorry we got off on the wrong foot. I'll be back later with the other brothers." His eyes flit around the room again. "Might consider cleaning up a bit before then. Believe it or not, I'm the most forgiving of the lot."

After Alec leaves, I shut the door and curse under my breath. I type out a quick text to Josh and just as I hit send, my phone starts ringing.

Mom.

Fuck. I am not in the mood for this. Hell, I'm still half asleep. But I answer anyway.

"Hey Mom."

"Clinton, baby?" she asks, sniffling.

"Mom?" My heart races in my throat. She's crying. "What's going on? Is Clayton okay?" She cries harder and I sink down onto the couch, my breath caught in my chest. "Mom?"

"He's fine, honey. I," she chokes out over a sob. "I need you to send me a little money, baby. I was stupid. I did some stupid shit and now I don't have money for Clayton's school fieldtrip and he doesn't have any lunch money and I barely have an ounce of food in the house. I know I was stupid, Clinton. Please don't penalize me. Please, baby, just help me out. Just this once."

As if the anger I had after Alec's morning visit wasn't enough, I feel it double in an instant. Heat rushes to my cheeks and I have to grip the arm of the couch to keep from punching something. "How much?"

"Just a little, baby."

"How. Much?"

She pauses, her voice growing smaller. "A hundred, maybe two."

I don't argue. I don't fight her. I don't have the energy to do either. "I'll text you with the confirmation." With that, I end the call, grab my keys, and head for the store. I'm gripping the wheel and driving too fast the entire way, but I can't calm myself down. I try texting Carleton, but he doesn't answer. Still. Letting out a frustrated growl, I throw my phone against the passenger side window and it bounces back into the seat.

I send her two hundred. I can't afford it, but I do it anyway. The thought of Clayton suffering at all makes me hate myself for leaving him behind. He should be here with me. Being only twelve, he's got a long time to go before he can leave on his own. Too long.

When I get back to the house, I change clothes and take off walking across campus toward the gym. I call Clayton when I'm halfway there and he answers on the second ring.

"Big bro!" he exclaims, his grin carrying through his voice. "What's up? How's Florida life?"

"Hot," I say with a chuckle, the sweat already

beading on my forehead. "How's Pennsylvania life?"

"Boring. But you already know how that goes."

I smile. "How's school? You feel any different being a seventh grader?"

"Well, the schoolwork still sucks. But the girls are filling out, if you know what I mean." He laughs through the receiver and I can't help but join him. That's my brother.

"Attaboy." My smile fades as I think about him not having food to eat. "Is everything okay at home, Clayton?"

There's a pause on the other end, but he answers after a beat. "Yeah. I mean, you know how she is. How everyone here is."

"Yeah. I know." Silence. "You know I love you, right? I'm always here for you. No matter what time of day."

"I know. I'm okay, bro."

"I know you are. You're tough."

"I learn from the best! But I have to go. I'm at Mac's and we're about to jump on Xbox. Call you later?"

"Sure thing, little bro. Kick his ass."

"Always!"

We end the call just in time for me to open the gym door. I feel broken. All I want is for Clayton to get the hell out of there and then we can both be done with our shitty family. But really, I know that's not true, either. Because there's still the boys. And even when Carleton and Mom pull their stupid stunts, they're still family. And blood runs thick.

I'm just not sure how much more I can give anymore.

BY THE TIME I limp my way back to the fraternity house, the sun is already setting. I didn't intend to stay at the gym all day but I wanted to numb myself. It worked, but I'm paying for it now and it'll be even worse tomorrow.

When I push my way through the front door, I'm met with thumping music and a packed house.

What the fuck.

"Josh!" I growl, catching sight of him first. I grab him by his shirt and yank him back toward the hallway where there are less people. "What the hell are you doing? Did you not get my voicemail earlier about the alumni?"

"Oh fuck them," he spits out. "They came by earlier, ripped us a new asshole, and then left.

They said they're moving our chapter meeting to tomorrow night, so we're getting in one last rage fest before the party police move in."

I sigh, but just like with Mom, I don't have the energy to argue. "Whatever." Releasing his shirt, I limp back to my room and jump in the shower, letting the hot water and steam melt away some of the tension from today. Then, against my better judgement, I join the party.

And I make it my mission to get hammered.

Before midnight even hits, I'm pinballing down the hallway with Lacy's mouth on mine. Lacy is a Zeta. She's small, almost doll-size, and her caramel skin against the bright white dress she's wearing are too much for me to handle. You would think with her wearing white to a frat party that she was trying to be innocent tonight. But with one hand under my basketball shorts, I know that's far from the truth.

"Fuck," she curses as I slam her back against my bedroom door. "Easy, Bear."

I suck and bite down her neck and toss her onto my bed with ease, pulling my shirt up and over my head at the same time. "I'm not doing easy tonight, babe. You either get me hard and rough or you don't get me at all. Your choice."

She swallows, but her lips part slightly and I can feel the want radiating off of her. When she doesn't answer, I fall down on top of her and slam my mouth on hers, hiking her leg up in the process. I know she's only a temporary numbing, just like the gym was earlier, but she's what I need. Sweat, alcohol, and sex. That's the distraction I'm looking for, and Palm South is the perfect place to find it.

I don't even bother taking off her dress or even the lacy thong I feel underneath it. I just quickly maneuver it to the side, roll on the condom I pulled from my top drawer, and thrust inside her in one fluid motion. She moans loud in my ear and it sends chills down my back. Thank God Josh likes the music loud.

"Oh God," Lacy screams, gripping my headboard as I slam into her over and over again. Her breasts are nearly tumbling out of her dress and her head hits against the board a little each time I thrust in.

"Nope, just me, babe."

I make sure she gets her release and as soon as she finishes, I lift both of her ankles up onto my shoulders and push deeper inside her pussy. She screams even louder and it doesn't take long for me to find my release, too. It completely numbs me and awakens every nerve at the same time. Finally, even if just for that moment, I don't think about anything else but the way it feels to come inside her.

When we finish, I make my way to the bathroom to flush the condom and then I fall back into bed, turning on my fan on my way over. I pull a pillow over my head to drown out the music and let my temporary euphoria drag me toward sleep. I don't know if Lacy stays and I honestly don't care. She can stay and sleep or she can leave. Right now, I'm not talking. Or cuddling. Or doing anything other than reveling in the fact that coming feels fucking amazing.

Before my thoughts have the time to sneak their way back in, I pass out.

Skyler

"YOU DON'T NEED TO SEND that much home to us, Skyler," my mom says softly and I can hear her tearing up a little.

"Mom. I want to. Please, just take it. It's not even that much."

"A thousand dollars is a lot of money."

"Well, it's not as much as I wish I could send."

Mom's silent, probably crying, so Dad takes his cue. They always talk to me on speaker phone. "We are so, so proud of you, honey."

I shrug. "It was just a little tournament, nothing to get too proud over."

"It is to us," he says. "And it may just be a small tournament now, but I know without a doubt that one day, you'll win tournaments so big you can't even imagine them right now."

"Whatever you say, Dad. Any word on that promotion?"

He pauses. "Not yet. I'm still holding out though."

I nod, but my gut tells me I should be worried. Mom and Dad both work in retail. Dad has been up for promotion to manager at least four times that I can remember, but his boss always screws him over. They do what they have to to make ends meet, but since neither of them finished high school, they don't have much to work with. But they work hard. *Damn* hard. And I'm determined to help them and maybe, one day, make it where they don't have to worry about working, at all.

"You'll get it, Dad. I know you will." I smile just as I key in the door code to the sorority house. "I just got home, I'm going to turn in. Love you guys."

"We love you too, sweetie," Mom replies through what are now clear sobs. I chuckle a little and end the call, stepping into the foyer. When I do, I nearly crash into Ashlei.

"Whoa!"

"Oh my God," she whisper-yells, clutching her chest. "You scared the shit out of me!"

"What are you doing? It's after three in the morning, Lei." I note her eccentric makeup and eye her curiously. She's dressed in what looks like pajamas, but clearly she wasn't sleeping. She, Jess, and Erin helped me get ready for the tournament earlier, much to my surprise, before Jess and Erin headed off to the social. But Ashlei said she couldn't go, so why was she covered in neon makeup?

Ashlei shifts under my gaze, adjusting the gym

bag on her shoulder. "Um, I went out. To a club downtown."

I cock a brow. "Really? With who? I thought you couldn't go out tonight."

She bites her lip, curses, and pulls me to the couch. "Listen, please don't say anything to Jess or Erin, okay? I had other plans tonight. That's why I couldn't go to the social."

"What other plans?" My brows rise higher.

"I can't tell you…"

"And why is that?"

She sighs. "Just, please, Skyler. Don't tell them and don't make a big deal about it. I was out with a few friends. That's all."

I study her for a moment more, but nod. "Okay, Lei. I won't say anything." She lets out a breath of relief. "Should I be worried, though?"

"No. I'm fine. Trust me."

"Okay." I nod again. "Well, I won the tournament tonight but I am exhausted. I'll see you in the morning?"

"Yeah," she says, smiling. "And congrats, Skyler. I may not understand the whole poker thing, but I know it's important to you. And I know what it's like to be worried about what others might think of the things that make you happy. So just know I'm proud of you."

I smile, but can't help but wonder how she knows what I feel like. Ashlei fits this sorority and all our friends like a glove. I'm not sure what she knows about worrying what others think of her. "Thanks, Lei. Love you."

She blows me a kiss and I scamper up the stairs to mine and Jess' room, quietly letting myself in and stripping down to my underwear before crawling into bed. Before I plug in my phone, I type out a quick text to Clinton. When no answer comes in after five minutes, I sigh and roll over toward the wall, pulling the covers up to my shoulders.

Something weird is going on with Clinton, and now Ashlei is acting strange, too. I know Jess is hiding something from all of us – something boy-related, if I had to guess. And Erin has barely spent more than ten minutes with me since classes started. I hate not knowing what's going on with my friends, and it hits me that maybe I need to stop focusing on distracting myself and start paying attention to the people around me, instead.

There are way too many secrets floating around PSU right now, and I'm determined to start uncovering them. It's time to hone in on my friends and reveal their truths.

Starting with Clinton.

Episode 3

"BUT IT COULD BE FUN, RIGHT?"

Ashlei

PULLING MY TIGHT spandex shorts out of my ass, I wipe down the pole and pat my hands together around a pinch of chalk. I don't usually chalk my hands before I work out – especially after seeing so many of my teammates start to rely on that method – but today, I need it. My palms are sweaty as hell.

There's a nervous pit in my stomach and I'm not sure if it's because the competition is less than a week away or if it's because I know what Hayden is doing behind the studio right now. Regardless, even with the chalk, I'm straining more than usual when I grip the pole and climb my way up, warming up with basic climbs and spins to keep my mind off everything else.

Skyler caught me sneaking in the house the other night and I know she's getting more and more curious about my whereabouts, which means I have to be extra careful. Pole dancing fitness isn't something you can easily explain to just anyone. Hell, I was a judgmental bitch when I first started learning about it. But then I met Hayden. Once he and Leslie started training me, I felt myself become addicted. Over the summer, I trained hard and used everything I learned from dancing my entire life to transfer into the moves on the pole. My flexibility made some of the moves almost natural for me, but building the body strength took time and patience. I'm proud of everything I've accomplished, but there's no way I can ever tell the girls about my hobby.

I'm pretty sure Erin would faint.

Jess would be pissed and say it's slutty.

Skyler would probably laugh and broadcast it across campus.

And my parents? Jesus… I can't even imagine.

No, I can't tell anyone. Sometimes, it's just

better to keep certain parts of your life separate from others.

"Damn girl," Hayden smacks my ass playfully just as I transition into my Russian splits.

I giggle and drop back down to my feet. "Way to break my focus."

Hayden pulls me into him for a long, sensual kiss that I feel all the way down between my thighs. "All part of the training, I swear." As much as I love the way his hands feel on me, I can tell he's high, and it turns me off as much as his tongue turns me on.

"Mm hmm. I'm sure." I push him away and climb back up. Leslie and Kya enter through the door he came through just moments ago and Leslie immediately starts warming up while Kya changes her shirt. Both of them are gorgeous, but Leslie is just downright hot. When I first met her, I was more attracted to her than I knew how to handle. I've always known I have a bisexual mindset, but I'd never really considered trying to openly hit on a girl until Leslie. That was, until Hayden stole my attention.

"Just us today?" I ask just before performing a simple drop.

"Only the ones who want to win, it looks like," Leslie answers. Her long, jet-black hair spins around her tight body as she warms up and I can't help but be temporarily mesmerized. The chick is still insanely hot, whether I'm with Hayden or not.

And I'm not even sure what we really are, anyway.

The South Florida Pole Dance Event is this Saturday and everyone in our troupe is entered in the competition. Leslie is the owner of Kitty Heels, our small-but-talented dance company, and she tells me every day that she could all but kiss Hayden for bringing me to them this summer. She sees potential in me, and this will be my first time to prove her right.

"You ready for your first competition, Ashlei?" Kya asks, her eyes shining in the flattering lighting of the studio. Kya is another star student of Leslie's. She's been dancing with Leslie since the beginning. Standing just shy of six feet and breaking that point in heels, she's the tallest girl in our troupe. But, she's also the strongest, and her moves are perfected to a point that I'm envious of. I'm not easily intimidated, but I'm threatened by her, for sure.

"Getting there." I answer, trying to feign confidence.

"You're going to be amazing," Hayden says, stretching on the floor by his pole. They brought

Hayden in a little over a year ago, but he seems to fit in perfectly. He's one of only two males in our entire studio and when he's on the pole, he's absolutely hypnotizing. His strength is out of this world. "When you bring home better awards than the rest of us, I expect a kiss of appreciation."

"And just where do you want this kiss, Hayden?" Leslie teases.

Hayden flashes his model grin. "I have a few ideas."

The girls chuckle and I drop to the floor long enough to toss my sweaty towel at him. Hayden Rivers is trouble walking. He's covered in beautiful tattoos, has a pierced eyebrow, and wears his shoulder-length hair back in a man bun that I swore I would never find attractive but did after the third time we hung out. He's lean, ripped in every muscle group from his neck to his ankles, and has just the slightest bit of facial hair. His piercing blue eyes top off his look and I swear he's the most exotic creature I've ever come in contact with. He's just as handsome as he is strange – and I love it.

He's also into hard drugs that Leslie doesn't know about, which makes me worry more often than I care to admit. But, he's a big boy – he makes his own decisions.

We run through our routines until we can barely stand anymore. By the time we finish, it's past midnight and I know I'll have to figure out a way to sneak back into the house again. Luckily, I room with Erin this year and she's always passed out by this time. With all her campus and sorority activities, she's exhausted by the time night rolls around and she sleeps heavier than anyone I know.

"Stay with me tonight," Hayden whispers into the back of my neck just as I pull a loose white t-shirt over my sports bra. He wraps his arms around my middle and pulls me back into him, pressing his hard on against my ass and forcing me to exhale a long, needy breath.

"I can't," I turn toward him, wrapping my arms around his neck. "I have class early in the morning and a sisterhood event tomorrow night. I have to get some sleep or I'm not going to make it."

"Sleep is overrated." He holds me tighter and nips up my neck to my earlobe, pulling it between his teeth. Hissing, I place my hands on his chest and try to put distance between us.

"You're killing me."

"I could be pleasuring you if you'd come home with me."

I push him off and grab my gym bag. "Goodnight, Hayden."

"Temptress," he teases, but he lets me go and I silently thank him for not trying again. Lord knows I can only say no to that kind of offer so many times.

When I climb into my little white Lexus SC convertible, my phone rings and I'm surprised to see Erin's name on the screen.

"Hello?"

"Where are you?! It's after midnight!" she yells into the receiver. At first I think she's scorning me, but then I realize it's exceptionally loud wherever she is and she has to yell over the noise.

Shit. The O Chi party.

"I... uh," I stammer, trying to figure out how to save my ass. I promised the girls I would go out to the Omega Chi Beta party tonight since I'd bailed on so much this semester. "I'm on my way. I got caught up working on this group project thing."

"Listen, if I'm up past my bedtime on a school night, you can blow off a group project," she jokes. "Get your ass here!"

"See you soon!"

I end the call and curse. All I want is a hot shower and my bed, but it looks like I'll have to settle for a quick shower and a frat party. I guess there are worse things I could be complaining about.

Running to the sorority house just long enough to rinse off and change, I make it to Omega Chi just after one. Erin and Jess find me as soon as I get through the door.

"About fucking time!" Jess yells. "Here, drink this." She shoves a red plastic cup full of beer into my hand and tips it up to my lips. Before she has the chance to spill any on me, I meet the lip of it with my mouth and drink. She's not satisfied until it's drained. "You have some catching up to do."

"I see that," I laugh the words, wiping beer from my lips. "Sorry I'm late."

"Whatever," Jess cuts me off. "Let's get hammered!"

Erin leans in to whisper to me. "I think someone already is."

We both giggle and start to follow Jess toward a game of flip cup in the next room when Clinton's booming voice carries from down the hallway.

"Just fucking drop it, Skyler!"

He emerges from the hallway just as Skyler tries grabbing his arm. He rips it away and turns to face her. Seething, he yells so loud it silences everyone else.

"It's none of your fucking business. If I wanted to talk to you about it, I would. But I don't, so leave me the fuck alone. Stop being so goddamn nosey!"

With that, he storms through the front door and slams it hard behind him.

Everyone is staring at Skyler, including us, but like a pro she doesn't miss a beat. Smiling, she shrugs. "Well damn. Anyone got a shot ready?"

The crowd laughs, although a little uneasily, and then the games resume and everything is back to normal. Skyler's eyes find ours and she makes her way across the room.

"What was that about?" Erin asks.

"It's nothing. He's fine, just stressed."

"He shouldn't talk to you like that, Skyler," Jess points out. "That's fucked up. Whatever has his panties in a wad, he didn't need to go all douchebag captain on you."

"It's all good. I'm fine." She turns to me and smiles. "And Lei is here! Let's drink!"

And we do. All night long. By the time we stumble our way into the house, I only have two hours to sleep before I have to be up for class. So much for sleep.

Tomorrow is going to be rough.

Adam

"SO I'LL SEE YOU there, right?" I ask the three freshmen girls standing in front of me. They all giggle and nod, their eyes flitting from the flier to me before they turn and walk away. I throw Jeremy a cocky grin and he just shakes his head.

"Only you could pull this off, you know that right?"

"Anyone could have before me," I say, handing a few fliers out to groups of students walking past our booth. "It's just that no one made the effort."

"That's because no one cared."

"And that's exactly why we're the lamest fraternity on campus," I deadpan.

"Touché." Jeremy chugs half of the water bottle in his hand and wipes his forehead. "Damn it's hot. Florida sucks."

"What's wrong, Michigan? Can't hang?"

He glowers at me before grabbing another stack of fliers. "Shut up or I'll make you do this shit by yourself."

"You'll make me flirt with every girl on campus to convince them to come to our concert? Wow. What a dick."

He flips me the middle finger before walking up to a group of Zetas. I laugh, but it's cut short when I spot our president making his way toward the tent.

Shit.

I'm not in the mood to put up with Clay, but I don't really have a choice. Out of all the brothers, he's the most resistant to the changes I want to make to our organization. In my opinion, he should have been doing all this a long time ago.

"So do we have a packed house for the concert yet?" he asks mockingly, eying our booth. I want nothing more than to smack that smug look off his face but I smile instead.

"Getting there. You want to help us pass out some fliers?"

"Nah, I'm on my way to the gym. Just wanted to see this shit show for myself." He snickers. "I can't wait to see this thing fail. Then maybe the alumni will realize why I didn't listen to you the first time you suggested it."

"Why are you against me on this?" I finally ask him, perturbed. "We're brothers, Clay. If we pack this concert, we'll put Alpha Sigma on the map again."

"We're on the map now."

I scoff. "You really are stupid if you honestly believe that."

His face drops and he steps forward, bowing up his chest to mine. "Maybe you should watch the way you speak to your president if you want to keep those letters."

I bite down on the inside of my cheek hard to keep from opening my mouth. Shaking my head, I don't give him another word before taking off toward a group of Omega Chi Betas. As much as we're rivals with them, we need their support just as much as the girls' at this event.

I'm still steaming over the conversation with Clay two hours later when Jeremy and I start breaking down the tent. It pisses me off that he can't stand to see me try to better our fraternity. Part of me thinks he's jealous or worried I'll overshadow him, and part of me knows he's just a miserable human being.

"Looks like I missed the party," a soft voice says behind me just as Jeremy and I pack the large navy tent into its cover. When I turn and come face to face with Cassie McBee, I smile.

"We can always take the party somewhere else."

"Oh yeah?" She grins. "Where to?"

Cassie is cute, I can't deny that, and part of me wants to tell her we can move whatever party she wants to my bedroom. But there's something about her that's innocent – too innocent for me to screw up. "Ralph's?"

Her face falls a bit, but she snaps out of it quickly. "Wish I could. I'm actually on my way to class."

"Let me walk you?"

"Uh," she falters, holding up the longboard I didn't realize she had tucked under her arm before.

"I didn't know you longboarded," I say, genuinely surprised. "Can't say I've met a sorority girl who rides before."

Cassie blushes. "Yeah well, I'm not initiated yet. Maybe the sorority girl life will wipe away my longboarding habits eventually."

"I hope not. But, can you ditch it long enough to let me walk you the rest of the way to class?"

"Sure."

I toss a glance at Jeremy to make sure he's cool with taking our equipment back. He nods and I grab a flier from our bag and hand it to Cassie as we turn away from the Student Union.

"Oh yeah, the concert," she assesses. "I already told you I'd be there."

"Just making sure you didn't forget. You bringing your slip-n-slide sister?"

She scrunches her nose in a way that makes her look even more innocent than before. "I don't like that nickname. But yes, she'll be there, too."

"What's wrong with that nickname?"

"I think it sends the wrong message." She waits for me to catch on and when I do, I blanch.

"I'm sorry, but that's hilarious. I like it even more now."

Cassie punches my arm lightly and I grin. Her bright scarlet hair is braided over her right shoulder, accenting the natural pink blush of her cheeks. I've never really been into red heads, but there's something about her that intrigues me.

The problem is, I feel the same way about her Big.

Skyler Thorne has always been a gorgeous girl, but getting to talk to her more this semester has piqued my interest. She's a spitfire and her confidence is unparalleled by any girl I know. Funny – it's like she and Cassie are almost polar opposites. One is innocent and light, one is mysterious and dark. They're like two sexy little devils perched on each one of my shoulders.

"This is me," Cassie says as we reach the

Sciences Building. "Will I see you before the concert?"

Her hazel eyes assess me and I throw her a sideways grin. "I'd be disappointed if you didn't."

When her cheeks flush red, I'm not sure how to feel about it, but I don't have time to analyze it before she turns and disappears behind the large wooden doors. Pulling out my cell, I type out a text to a few brothers to meet at the house. We have a lot to get done before next weekend and I'm determined to do it right.

Alpha Sigma may be in the back of everyone's minds now, but if I have anything to do with it, we'll be all the campus can talk about by the end of the semester.

Erin

"I CAN'T BELIEVE this will be your last initiation," I say to Siomara, hugging one of her chevron square pillows close to my chest. "You're graduating, G-Big. That's insane."

Siomara smiles, her white teeth blazing against her dark Spanish skin. "I still have a couple of months."

"It's just crazy," I whisper, shaking my head. "And then you'll be president, Big." I turn to Kelsey. Her soft grin spreads into a full-blown smile and she looks to Siomara.

"If I get voted in."

"Like it's even a question." Kelsey has been training for this moment since she became a KKB sister. Regardless of the fact that everyone in our Greek family line for the past seven years has been president, Kelsey is literally the only candidate for the position. She's incredibly driven, smart, and talented. If anyone can lead our sorority and make it even better than it is now, it's her.

"Speaking of which, how do you feel about our newest family addition, Ex?" Siomara asks.

"She's really sweet. Quiet, kind of shy, but when she's around Skyler she seems to open up."

"Have you had the chance to connect with her one on one?"

My mouth pulls to the side. "Honestly, I've been so busy I really haven't."

"Erin," Kelsey scolds me. "She's your Grand Little. Don't you want to have the same relationship with her that you have with Siomara?"

"Ugh, I suck," I groan. "Sometimes I get so wrapped up in all the event planning that I forget to be a good friend. Or in this case, a good Grand Big."

Siomara pats my back sympathetically. "Don't let yourself drown in the logistics of it all. At the end of the day, this is still college and these four years are supposed to be full of amazing fun. Don't let friendship fall second to leadership."

"Wow, so deep, Big," Kelsey teases. Siomara sticks her tongue out and continues making notes in our initiation guidebook.

"Just make some time for her, okay? She's new to all this. Once we initiate her, she'll be a sister for life. Help her understand what an awesome thing that is," Siomara adds. I nod and we get back to work, prepping everything for the ceremony and the celebration after.

Maybe it's the Greek family line I was brought into or maybe it's just my inherent nature to always be a super nerd, but our sorority ceremonies have always been close to my heart. I love planning them, and I love seeing new sisters experience them even more. There's something magical when we're all singing or reciting principles that were founded more than one-hundred years ago that gives me chills. So many people judge Greek life and claim it's "buying friends". If only they were open-minded enough to see what it's really about.

Friendship.

Family.

Scholarship.

Community.

And so much more.

Taking Siomara's advice, I text the girls and ask them all to meet me at Ralph's when we finish initiation practice. I'm applying the last bit of liner to my almond-shaped brown eyes when my phone rings.

"Hey Mom," I answer, putting her on speaker phone so I can finish up my makeup. My medium-length blonde hair is a tangled mess so I pull it up into a high pony and let a few strands hang, framing my face.

"Erin, dear, how are you?" My mom's voice is like a mixture of milk and honey – smooth, with a thick southern drawl.

"I'm well. I'm actually about to head out with the girls, can I give you a call tomorrow?"

"Please tell me you're behaving in a lady-like manner, Erin Xander," she warns. "You don't want to get yourself a reputation."

Fighting the urge to roll my eyes, I suck my lips between my teeth and think before responding. "I have a great reputation on campus, Mom. Don't worry."

"I hope so. For how much your father and I donate to the school, you know you have eyes on you at all times. And let's not forget you'll be a senior next year." Her voice trails off, but she doesn't need to finish the sentence for me to pick up what she's implying. My parents expect me to find a "suitable man" to date by next year so I can be engaged right after I graduate. I want law school, they want an MRS degree – Mrs. Rich Ass Doctor.

"Mom, you know I'm going to be president, which means I'll be here an extra semester. And regardless of how you and Dad try to ignore me when I say it, I want to go to law school."

"Oh Erin," she says with a sad sigh. "You're much too pretty to be a lawyer."

I don't even try to argue. "I have to go, Mom. Talk soon."

"Okay, darling. Kisses."

Suddenly, my need for a drink escalates from an eight to an eleven.

My parents are from what I've always known as "old money". They both come from rich parents who also come from rich parents. None of the women in my family have ever worked a day in their life, unless you count fitness and party-hosting as work. My mom was hesitant to even entertain my idea of getting a degree at all, but conceded only when she realized I'd probably need to go to college if I wanted to meet a doctor or an entrepreneur.

I may be the only girl in the country whose parents would be disappointed if I passed the BAR.

When I get to Ralph's, Skyler, Cassie, Bo, and Jess are already waiting at a back table. It's happy hour, so I slide up to the bar and grab a cheap plastic cup filled with beer before heading back to them.

Mother would be so proud.

"Let me guess," I say, chugging half my beer before taking a seat next to Bo. "Lei was busy again?"

"We shouldn't be worried, right?" Skyler asks, her brows furrowed.

"Why would we be?" Jess challenges. We all turn to Skyler, waiting. She looks uneasy, like maybe she said something she shouldn't have.

Shrugging us off, she grabs her drink and lifts it to her lips. "I don't know. No reason. I'm just being weird."

No one pushes the subject, but when I see Jess sketchily glaring at some bald guy across the room, I decide it's the perfect time to call her out. "Speaking of weird, what's going on with you and teacher guy?" I waggle my brows and Jess groans.

"He's annoying."

"Oh?" Bo chimes in. "So you're not into him anymore?"

"Oh I'm still *very* into him."

We all exchange blank stares.

"He's annoying because he won't go the fuck away." She groans. "I'm not allowed to have him, yet he has to look sexy as hell in class every day and then he somehow happens to party at the same bars, too. I mean really," she dramatically gestures toward where the bald guy she was just staring at is seated at the bar. I guess that's Jarrett. "How unfair is it that he looks that good right now and I'm three drinks past buzzed?"

"Just go talk to him," Skyler urges, being

her normal, confident self. "I mean seriously, he probably wants to bone, too."

"No way," Jess argues, shaking her head. "You should see the pained looks he gives me in class. Like I'm the biggest regret he has and he's just waiting for my ticking time bomb to go off and expose his shit."

We all fall silent, unsure of how to argue that. If I were Jarrett, I'd be worried about Jess blabbing, too. He has more to lose. He has *everything* to lose.

Suddenly, a wide grin breaks out on Bo's face. "Well look who decided to show."

Ashlei gives her a pointed look. "Talking shit about me, girls?"

"Always," Skyler jokes, cheersing Ashlei's fresh cup of beer. "Looks like you have some catching up to do again."

"Well," she concedes, lifting her cup as we all do the same. "I guess it's a good thing I like a challenge."

Ashlei

SITTING AT THE SORORITY HOUSE is driving me insane. I don't feel prepared for the competition tomorrow, but there's nothing more I can do. I practiced all day and if I do any more, I'm going to be too sore and worn out to compete. This is the time when I'm supposed to rest and prep my body, but all I feel is anxiety.

Ever since I can remember, I've always been competitive. And not just a little bit, but to a fault. I blame my need to win for all my failures in dance throughout the years. I would constantly push myself too hard and then punish myself if I didn't win. I even went through a cutting phase, which I knew was wrong and hurtful and stupid but I did it anyway. Now, I'm older. I'm more mature and I've learned from my past.

But I still feel that same need to win overpowering every other sense right now.

"What I would give to get inside that pretty head of yours," a sweet voice says in the darkness. I jump, but relax when Bo's smiling face comes into focus. She joins me on the small white porch swing set up in the back courtyard of our house and I return her smile.

"Trust me, you don't want to know everything going on in my head right now."

"Actually, I do. And I'm not the only one." Her brows pull together. "Everyone is talking about you, you know. The way you're always dodging events, the weird makeup, the late nights." She shrugs. "Some of us are worried."

The way she says that last part does something to my stomach that I know isn't good. Bo is stunning, and more than that – she's unique. Not just with her petite stature and exotic features, but with her sharp tongue and gentle heart, too.

"You guys don't need to worry about me."

"Well," she says, chewing her cheek. "Maybe if you tell me what you're up to, I can help ease the tension in the group."

Her dark brown eyes are almost black in the low lighting of the courtyard. With her hair pulled over one shoulder and her kind smile, she radiates beauty in the simplest way imaginable.

"I can't tell you, Bo. I can't tell anyone."

Bo frowns. "Are you in trouble?"

"No," I answer honestly. "Promise."

"Tell me anything," she tries again. "Whatever you feel like you *can* tell me."

I sigh, struggling with my inner voice telling me I need to keep my mouth shut and my inner anxiety fighting to tell someone – anyone – about the competition.

"Let's just say… I have a unique hobby. I love it, I'm good at it, and tomorrow I'm going to be…" My voice trails off as I struggle for the right words. "Tested on it."

Bo looks confused, but she doesn't press for more. "Well, whatever it is, I can tell you're stressed about it." I nod, but then she places her soft hand over mine on the edge of the swing. My breath catches and her eyes flick to mine. Swallowing, she pulls her hand back. "But you shouldn't be, Lei. You're amazing. At everything you do. And whatever this thing is that you can't tell us about, I can tell it's important to you. I know you're going to pass whatever test it is that you have tomorrow because that's the kind of person you are. You're a winner."

For a moment, I don't respond. The air around us feels different from when she first joined me on the swing and I can't figure out how to comprehend the change. "Thank you," I finally manage just above a whisper.

Bo nods, then she lifts herself from the swing. "I'm going to make some tea. You want some?"

"Yeah, actually that sounds great."

"Come on." She notions inside and I follow, possibly watching her a little more closely than I should. Before this semester, Bo Hán was just my best friend's Little.

But now, I have a troubling feeling that I might want her to be more.

"OH MY FUCKING FUCK!" Leslie screams when we all pile back into our private dressing room. The entire troupe is jumping up and down, trophies and medals in hand. The energy is uncontrollable.

"I seriously can't believe this," I chime in, shaking my head. "We won. First place. In four categories!"

"Well believe it," Hayden says, picking me up and twirling me in his arms. "And I think we can all agree that we have you to thank." He plants a long kiss on my lips.

"It was all of us. We're a team."

"True," Kya says, unfastening her bra. I used to be shocked by how comfortable she was stripping in front of anyone and everyone, but I'm used to it now. "But we've all competed before and we've never done this well. You kicked ass today, Ashlei."

She winks and strips off her spandex, quickly replacing it with a pair of fitted sweats.

"To Ashlei," Leslie says, pulling a flask from her Kitty Heels gym bag. We all chuckle as she takes a swig and begins to pass it around. Various members of the troupe clap me on the back in congratulations after they take their swigs. Then, everyone starts getting dressed, energy still buzzing around us.

"Hey," Hayden says, grabbing my hand. "Come with me. I have a better way to celebrate." He winks and a roaring fire instantly lights in my stomach.

Pulling me through the dressing room to a back bathroom, he locks the door behind us and props me up on the counter, pressing himself between my thighs in one quick motion. Slowly, he kisses down my neck, his strong hands gripping my hips as he does. He's still in the tight, barely-there shorts from our final routine and nothing else. I drag my fingernails down over his chest and abs before tucking them beneath the thin fabric. Even though I just barely graze him, I can feel how hard he is and I bite my lip in anticipation.

"Wait," he breathes, pecking my lips once more before backing up slightly. When he pulls a small plastic bag filled with white powder out of one of the bathroom cabinets, I immediately shake my head.

"No, Hayden. No way. You know I'm not into that stuff."

"Come on," he says sexily, his voice low and his eyes bright. "We just won in four categories. We qualified for semi-finals in January. Celebrate with me. Just one line. I promise, I'll take care of you. I won't let anything happen. It's just going to make you feel even more alive than you already do."

I bite my lip, feeling my heartrate accelerating. I know I shouldn't, but the way Hayden is looking at me makes me want to. I'm already on a high, I *do* want to celebrate, and I do trust Hayden. I know he won't let anything bad happen to me.

But I know cocaine is no joke.

But it could be fun, right?

But I shouldn't do it…

Sensing my inner battle, Hayden moves toward me and slowly shakes some of the white powder onto my cleavage. Using a small blue plastic card, he situates it into a clean line and then looks up at me with heated eyes. He shoots the line, then takes my mouth with his in a frenzy, igniting the desire in my body again.

When he pulls back, he gently empties out a small amount of powder onto his strong trapezius muscle and situates it in a clean line. Then, he hands me the small metal pipe. "Just a little bit, Ashlei. Come up with me," he pleads. I just sit there with the pipe in my hand, staring at the line and telling myself I should hand the pipe back to him. But something inside me is curious.

Hayden bites his lower lip, letting his teeth drag across the flesh before trailing his hand down my abdomen to land between my thighs. When his fingers snake their way through the fabric and plunge inside of me, I let out a sharp cry of pleasure and let myself fall back against the mirror.

"Come up with me, Ashlei," he says again, working his magical fingers inside me. The ecstasy is already too much, I can't imagine it any more heightened. But with Hayden's hooded eyes devouring me right along with his hands, I can't find the energy to argue anymore. Leaning up, I take a deep breath, plug one nostril, and shoot the line off his bare flesh.

It stings like hell and my eyes water as I wipe my nose, but Hayden is looking at me like I'm the sexiest thing he's ever seen. He steals the pipe from my hand and tosses it on the counter before pulling my mouth to his. While his other hand still works beneath my outfit, the other grips the back of my neck, pulsing a need straight through me.

Suddenly, Hayden pulls my spandex off and rips his to the floor, leaving us both exposed. He teases me at my entrance with his head, nipping playfully at my bottom lip. "You're so fucking sexy, Ashlei. This is going to feel amazing. Trust me."

With that, he plunges into me and I let out a loud moan. At first, I don't feel any different, but after a few minutes, everything changes. I feel incredibly alert, my senses extra-sensitive, and the pleasure I normally feel when Hayden touches me is amplified to a level I've never experienced before. Each time he thrusts into me, every time his thumb brushes my nipple, each flick of his tongue on my skin sends me spiraling toward a dangerous cliff of ecstasy.

"This feels amazing," I moan into Hayden's lips. "*Everything* feels so amazing."

"Like this?" he asks, palming each of my breasts. I nod and grind my pelvis against his as he works in and out. "And this?" he asks again, this time letting his fingertips fall to circle my clit. My moans grow louder and it's my only response before I tumble over the edge and experience an orgasm I never knew existed. It takes over my entire body, my entire soul, my entire being. And when I finish, I'm spent. Completely, totally spent. Crashing, fading, falling.

Hayden comes moments later and then he pulls me into one of the showers with him, planting small kisses down the back of my neck as he runs his hands through my wet hair. Even as the high fades, every touch sparks my sensitive skin and I feel alive. But slowly, the guilt starts to creep in along with the realization of what just happened. Before today, alcohol and the occasional joint were the only drugs I'd ever messed with. Now, I've jumped over the fence into hard drug territory. It was electrifying, it was terrifying, but what scares me most is...

It was fun.

Adam

THERE'S NOTHING QUITE LIKE the feeling of seeing something you've worked hard for pay off. You bust your ass for weeks, months, or maybe even years and then it all comes together and you finally feel like you can breathe again.

That's how I feel right now as I stare up at the big stage while a local band kills their set and the crowd goes crazy. Crowd. Yeah, there's actually a big turnout at an Alpha Sigma event. I shake my head, still shocked I somehow pulled it off, and glance down at my clipboard.

"Okay, Filthy Innocents are wrapping up. Give our headliner the five minute warning," I say into the mouthpiece wrapped around my head.

"Ten four," Jeremy answers and I roll my eyes.

"You don't have to talk like a fucking trucker, Jeremy."

"Ten four."

As I make my way across the crowded lawn to the stage, I spot Skyler, Cassie, and a group of their sorority sisters close to the front row. It's Cassie I notice first, her scarlet hair standing out in the crowd of brunettes and blondes. She's dressed in a tight little green dress that takes my eyes down her body whether I try to fight it or not. Which I don't, by the way. She looks great tonight, and she's definitely the one I noticed first.

But it's Skyler who keeps my attention.

A stark contrast from her sisters, she's in distressed jeans and her sorority jersey. Her hair is pulled up into a messy bun and even though I can tell she has makeup on, it doesn't look like she tried as hard as her sisters to look as amazing as she does.

Fucking Christ, the girl is gorgeous.

"Well if it isn't the –"

"Don't even say it," Cassie cuts me off, shoving me playfully as Skyler and the rest of the girls turn around. The three blondes, one I know to be Erin Xander and the other two I'm not familiar with, give me a onceover before turning back toward the stage. Skyler's eyes, however, stay fixed on mine.

"You know, I can honestly say you surprised me tonight."

I cock a brow. "Oh?"

"Yep," she nods. "I did not think A Sigs could get down like this. I'm impressed."

"Me too," Cassie chimes in, her cheeks flushing a bit with the words. It's not lost on me, and I can't say it doesn't give me a thrill to know that blush is because of me.

"Let's get a drink before the headliners go on," one of the blondes says, grabbing Skyler's arm before turning to Cassie.

"I'll save our spot," she says. The girls all nod and squeeze their way past me toward the Alpha Sigma house where the open bar is. It's an illegal open bar, one the campus coordinators wouldn't approve as part of the concert, but I knew without booze this show would go down in flames. So, our basement was transformed into a speakeasy.

"I'll stay with you." Cassie turns to me wide-eyed and I flash a smile. "It's the least I can do, since I'm assuming it was probably you who got all your sisters here."

She flushes a deeper red. "It didn't take much to convince them. Music. Food. Booze. And boys."

"Which of those did you come for?"

She gulps. "The first one… mostly."

I grin. "How's your first semester going?"

"It's good." I can tell by her hesitance there's something she's not saying. "Lots of parties and sorority events. I'm having fun."

"But?"

"But what?" She looks at me confused.

"You're upset about something."

"Why do you say that?"

I shrug. "I can just tell."

Sighing, she looks down and picks at her nail polish. "It's nothing, really. I just… I moved here with my best friend. We both rushed together, but she went Zeta. Ever since rush, she's been a mega bitch and it's just getting worse every day. She doesn't understand why I went KKB and she thinks Zetas are better. She keeps pulling away from me and I feel like I'm going to lose her this semester if I haven't already."

"Is she really that great of a friend if she's treating you like this?"

"She used to be. I don't know, maybe this is just the whole growing up thing. I just miss the girl I knew a few months ago."

I lean in closer, speaking over the sound of instrument tuning and mic checks. "People change, Cassie. You're going to notice in the next few years and probably for the rest of your life that some friends stay and some friends go. The trick is learning that real friendships don't have to be fought for."

She smiles, looking up at me through her lashes. In the bright blue and green lights of the concert, she looks sort of angelic. And I know she kind of is – she's innocent in a way I've never seen a girl before.

Suddenly, there's a surge in the crowd as the lights go down and Cassie is knocked forward hard. When she smacks into me, she apologizes, but I just grab her arms to steady her. "You okay?" She nods, but then suddenly the air around us is thicker than before. Her body is pressed against mine and I can feel the slightest hint of shaking as I hold her. Before I know what I'm doing, I lower my mouth to hers, our lips touching just as the first notes of the new set play.

She sighs into my mouth and I pull her closer, parting her lips with my tongue and moving my hands up to cup her face. Her hands fist my shirt and a soft, almost inaudible moan escapes when I dip my tongue in again. It's then that I realize what I'm doing.

I pull back, pressing my forehead to Cassie's. Then I laugh. What the hell am I doing?

"Man, I'm so sorry. That was weird, huh?"

Cassie pulls all the way back.

"I don't know why I did that. I guess I'm just caught up in all the excitement tonight. I hope this won't make anything weird between us." I rub the back of my neck with one hand and shove the other in my pocket. This chick is one of the coolest I've met at Palm South and of course I let my penis talk me into fucking up that friendship.

Cassie bites her lip, her brows pulled together. I can't tell if I really wigged her out or if she's still trying to register what happened. "No, uh, no. Not weird at all."

I let out a breath I didn't know I was holding. "Good. I really like hanging out with you, Cassie. I didn't mean to take it there."

"It's not, you didn't," she stammers, shaking her head. "It's all good. You were just excited. Zero weirdness, I promise."

I pull her in for a hug just as the girls join us again. "Thanks. I have to run backstage. See you after the show?"

"Yeah. See you."

I turn to leave, still shaking my head at how idiotic I am when Skyler grabs my arm.

"Hey, do you have a thing for my Little?"

I glance at Cassie behind her, but her eyes are fixed on the stage. "No. She's cool, though. I like her, but as a friend."

Skyler nods. "Okay."

Once more, she grabs my arm as I try to leave.

"I just had to clear that up before I did this."

"Did what?"

She runs her soft hand down my arm, her blue eyes dazzling in the rave lights as she tucks something into my front pocket. I swallow when she does, her hand falling way too close to a part of my body she awakened earlier tonight.

"My number," she answers the question I haven't even asked yet. "Call me tonight." With that, she winks and rejoins the girls, not even giving me a second look.

I jog backstage with a shit-eating grin on my face, but it's knocked off almost immediately.

"This concert sucks," Clay says, draining the rest of the dark liquid in his water bottle. From his breath, I assume it's whiskey.

"Don't be a prick, Clay." I shove past him, ordering a few of our brothers to get everything ready for the finale.

"It does. These bands are all local. No one gives a shit."

"Well, there's about a thousand people out there that say you're wrong."

"Whatever. I'm embarrassed that our name is associated with this mess."

Clenching my jaw, I whip around to face him again. "What the fuck is your problem? Are you worried, Clay?" I know I'm crossing a line I shouldn't, but I don't care, even with Jeremy grabbing my shoulder in warning. "Afraid someone might notice what a shit president you are and vote someone else in who actually gives a fuck?"

"And what?" he challenges. "You think that someone is you?"

"Maybe." I stand tall, and Jeremy finally drops his hand, giving up.

Clay stares at me for a moment, then he lets out a guttural laugh, leaning over and bracing his hands on his knees. Clenching my teeth, I surge toward Clay but Jeremy holds me back.

"It's not worth it, man," he mutters.

"I'd listen to him, Brooks," Clay says through his laughter. "You may not want me to be, but I'm still your president. And I can have you kicked out of this fraternity faster than you come in bed. And that's saying something."

I rush forward again, but this time more hands join Jeremy's and they all hold me back. Clay chuckles once more before turning and disappearing into the crowd.

"Don't let him ruin your night, man," Jeremy says. "He's just being a dick. He's mad he didn't think of this first and he's even more upset that you actually pulled it off."

I know he's right, I know it's jealousy – but he's still a fucking prick who deserves to have his jaw broken. Shaking Jeremy off, I nod and check the set list. One song away from the finale. "Let's do this."

In the middle of the last song, just as the music builds, two cannons shoot neon confetti over the black light crowd and the lights strobe in time with the beat. The crowd goes crazy, fog machines mixing with the confetti and the lights. It's exactly the ending I wanted, everyone's going nuts, but I can't even fucking enjoy it.

Then, through the fog, I spot Cassie. She's looking up at the confetti falling, a wide-eyed look on her face. She looks happy, and that makes me feel like maybe it's okay for me, too. I may not be innocent like she is, but I've worked my ass off for this moment.

Grabbing one of the bottles of champagne lined up backstage, I run out into the crowd with Jeremy and several other brothers following. I shake the bottle and open it quickly, spewing the liquid everywhere as more people scream and jump in time with the music. The feeling coming from the crowd is electrifying and the band feeds off of it, making the show even better than I could have imagined.

Clay may have power over me now, but something tells me it won't be that way for much longer.

Erin

MY HEART IS FULL. I don't know how else to describe it.

I thought initiation as a Big was special, but seeing Skyler pin Cassie during our initiation brought an entirely new kind of pride to my heart. I watched as each of the new girls listened to our founding principles, committing them to memory and swearing to keep them secret for life. Their eyes were wide, their expressions eager – it was an amazing sight to behold.

For me, it always seems too short. We've been preparing for weeks, but already the ceremonial clothing is packed away, along with the candles and ritual books, and sisters are scattered around the hotel venue taking photos with their lines. Spotting my line, I pull my phone from my Kate Spade purse.

"Cheese!" I snap the photo before any of them have the chance to realize what I'm doing and they all groan in unison.

"Not fair!" Kelsey shrieks.

"Seriously this time," I say, grouping them together. I find another sister to take our photo and jump in right behind Skyler. We make a long line, starting with Siomara at the top standing on a chair and ending with Cassie on her knees. Our family tree is one of the biggest in the sorority, since Siomara stays an extra semester to be president. I love the feeling of being the largest and, in my opinion, the best.

After a dozen photos at the fountain and around the hotel garden, I steal Cassie away from the group.

"So, you're officially a sister," I say, grinning. "Do you feel different?"

Her smile is just as big as mine and I have a feeling she'll be more like me than Skyler. She seems to have that same passion for history that I do. "Honestly, yes. I really do. And I wasn't expecting that."

"It's amazing, isn't it?"

She nods. "I have to admit, I was a little creeped out at the beginning. The dark room… candles… weird clothing."

I laugh, nudging her. "Trust me, I was freaked out too. But you have to think, that ceremony was created in the late eighteen hundreds."

"That gives me chills. How awesome to think how many sisters we have across the states."

"Across the world," I correct her. Cassie smiles wider and we walk the grounds of the hotel, talking about her roommate, classes, and a little about my family. I don't go into full detail, but I give her a little sneak into my parents and their craziness. Her family seems to be the polar opposite of mine – loving, supportive, kind.

It makes me envy my Grand Little.

When we make our way back to the lobby where all the sisters are waiting for our charter bus, I notice Skyler is missing.

"Where'd Sky go?" I ask Siomara.

"She said she had some errands to run but that she'd see us at Ralph's later."

"Oh. Want to grab dinner, Cassie? We can go back to the house and get ready for Ralph's afterward."

"Yes!" she answers excitedly. "I'm starved."

Siomara and Kelsey join us for dinner at the sushi restaurant on campus. Glancing around the table at my sisters, I feel an overwhelming warmth envelop me. In high school, I was lost. I went through so much that no one ever knew about – not even my parents. It was the summer before my senior year when I found myself, and ever since then, I've thrown myself into everything I love – this sorority being one of those things.

Some people go to college for the education, some for the parties, some to find love. Me? Well,

I guess I want all of those things, too – but more than anything, I want memories. I want friendship. And I know without a doubt that I've found both in Kappa Kappa Beta.

WE'RE STILL LAUGHING as we pile into the sorority house, Kelsey and Siomara heading up to the President Bedroom while Cassie and I made our way to my room.

"Do you need to borrow clothes or did you bring some?"

Cassie's mouth pulls to the side. "I didn't bring any. Would you mind letting me borrow something?"

"Of course not! Come on," I lead her up the stairs. "I have the perfect outfit for you."

I help Cassie dress in tight, dark jeans and a slinky black top with an open back before pulling out a simple red dress for me. I can tell Cassie is new to the dressing up thing – almost as new as Skyler was last year when she rushed. But, at least Cassie has some grasp on makeup and what to pair with an outfit. Skyler is clueless. She'd much rather be in ratty jeans and a t-shirt and, more often than

I care to see, she does end up in that. But, when it comes to something important, she lets us dress her.

Thank God.

"I feel like it's missing something," Cassie says, staring at her reflection in the full-length mirror.

"Hmm… Oh! We need a pop of color. Skyler has some killer red heels she wore for some poker thing last semester. Let's go steal them from her. Pair those with some red lipstick and you're set!"

Giggling as we rush down the hallway to her room, we burst through the door and flick on the lights.

"Shit!" A voice says from beneath the covers on Skyler's bed. Her head pops out and she's completely flushed, her hair a mess and her makeup smeared. There's someone else in the bed with her, but they won't reveal themselves.

"Are you fucking serious, Skyler?!" I yell, but quickly close the door behind Cassie. Lowering my voice, I storm to the bed and rip the covers back, revealing the guy from the Alpha Sigma concert. "You have got to be kidding me. I know you did not bail early on initiation to bring a BOY back to the sorority house. Mom Cindy will literally skin you alive if she finds out!"

"Well, she doesn't have to if you stop

screaming!" Skyler whispers, giggling. The man in her bed is attractive, I'll give her that. His dark hair is messy, but his even darker eyes are hooded with lust. Pair all that with his charming grin and I can see why she brought him back.

"Okay, you have two minutes to get him dressed and out of here."

"Um," she pauses, looking to the guy. "Could we maybe get like five?"

"Oh my God just get him out!" I throw the covers over both of them, grab her red heels from the bottom of her closet, and lead Cassie back to my room. I'm chuckling a little as we reach my door.

"Your Big," I start, tossing her the heels. "She's something else, that one."

Cassie's face is sheet white. "Yeah."

"Are you okay?" I rush to her side. "Oh crap, did you eat bad sushi?"

"I'm fine." Cassie slips on the heels as she hops into the bathroom. "Just let me put on some lipstick and I'll be ready."

"Perfect. I don't know about you, but I'm ready for a drink. You have your fake, right?"

"Yeah," she says, finishing the last coat of red on her lips. She packs the lipstick in her clutch and turns back to me, a new determination on her face.

"And I don't just need *a* drink. I need ten."

"Now you're talking like a KKB!"

I throw my arm around her shoulder, steering her out the door. Just as we reach the bottom of the stairs, the front door flies open and Ashlei stumbles through.

She's still in her initiation dress, but the white fabric is wrinkled and stained in several places now. Her skin is covered in a light sheen of sweat and I can tell without a second glance that she's been crying.

"Oh my God. Ashlei, what happened?"

Ashlei's eyes are empty as they meet mine. She gazes around the foyer for a moment before closing the front door behind her and stumbling toward the stairs. "I'm fine. I'm skipping Ralph's."

She starts making her way up and Cassie and I exchange worried glances. "Ashlei," I call out, following her. Cassie is on my heels. "You're clearly not fine. What's going on?"

"I said I'm fine!" she screams, turning on me. "God, Erin, you're not my mother. Back off!" With that, she runs the last few stairs and a few seconds later I hear the door to our room slam shut. Swallowing, I turn back to Cassie.

"Do you want to stay with her?" she offers.

"No, no. She won't talk to anyone when she's like that. Let's just go. I'll talk to her in the morning."

Cassie offers a soft smile and nods.

Regardless of the tension at the house, Cassie and I loosen up once we get to Ralph's. Jess and Bo are already there and Skyler joins us not too long after, looking satisfied and ready to party. Jess high fives her when she finds out what happened and Bo buys her a shot. I can only shake my head.

Initiation is over. The semester is halfway over, too. Looking around the bar at my sisters, I feel the heaviness of that settle in on me. Something is going on with Ashlei, Skyler's hiding something with Bear, Jess is skating on thin ice with a teacher and my parents are on my ass more than ever. Sighing, I sip on my shitty college-bar martini. I don't have much time to think on all the drama, though, because Jess and Skyler jump up on the bar and start pouring shots straight out of the bottle into the mouths of students lining the barstools. I let out a laugh and raise my glass.

The KKB girls may be kind of crazy, but I wouldn't have it any other way.

Episode 4

"I DIDN'T PEG YOU FOR A GOOD GIRL"

Cassie

IT'S STRANGE HOW SOME MEMORIES are fleeting, almost gone the moment they happen, and others are burned into our brains and locked on replay. The kiss I shared with Adam just a little over a week ago is one of the latter. Lying in the hot South Florida sun right now only seems to sear the impression of his mouth onto mine even more. I'm not sure I'll ever be able to lick my lips again without tasting his.

"Seriously, why would anyone want to live anywhere other than Florida?" Jess asks with a sigh, leaning back into her beach chair further. "It's a Tuesday. In late October. And we're on the beach."

"One of the many perks of Palm South," Erin adds, sipping on the vodka water mix she has in her Kappa Kappa Beta tumbler cup. Jess, Erin, and Ashlei are still tan from the summer and each little bit of sun they've managed to catch since fall hit. My skin, on the other hand, never seems to stray too far from a pale white. Sometimes I get tan lines, but usually they're more like *peach* lines. I don't ever get truly tan.

"Where's your Big, Cassie?" Jess asks. I steal a glance at Ashlei through my shades. She's been quiet all day, barely saying more than a few words. She just keeps steadily sipping on her own tumbler and staring out at the waves.

"Skyler had to practice for that tournament she's in this weekend. I've barely seen her since initiation." I gulp, remembering exactly the way I saw her that night – tangled up in the sheets with Adam.

"Boo," Jess resolves. "I don't think I'll ever understand her obsession with that game."

"I think there's more to it than she tells us." I notice Erin avoiding the conversation when I hint to Skyler holding something back and it only confirms it. There's something she's not telling us.

Seems to be a lot of that going on around here.

"I'm going in the water." Ashlei doesn't wait for anyone to respond before she's up out of her chair and halfway to where the gentle waves are rolling in.

"Is she okay?" I ask, not really pointing the question to anyone directly.

"She hasn't really talked to me since we ran into her before Ralph's on Saturday," Erin answers, her mouth pulled to the side. "Ashlei is really private, though. She'll tell us what's on her mind when she's ready." Erin turns to me. "How's the situation with your roommate, G-Little?"

I groan. "Awful. I can't wait to move into the sorority house next semester. I don't want to lose my relationship with Paris but I swear she couldn't care less if I was eaten by a shark."

"What's her deal, anyway? Weren't you best friends in high school?" Jess asks, reapplying lotion to her shoulders.

"That's what makes it so difficult. She's completely different and we've only been here two months. I don't understand it." I frown and sip on my own drink, enjoying the buzz of day drinking in the sunshine. It's an entirely different kind of tipsy than a bar at night.

"Oh my God." Jess fumbles with her drink, trying to pull her large, floppy beach hat over her face. "Shit. Shit shit shit."

"What?" Erin and I ask in unison.

"It's Jarrett. Fuck! How is it that this guy is everywhere I am?! I know our campus is small but Jesus Christ."

Just as she says the words, I spot Jarrett down the beach. His bald head is covered with a baseball cap pulled on backward and his eyes are shielded behind thick black sunglasses. Even from this distance I can see a plethora of tattoos sprawling up both of his arms.

"Damn, Jess," Erin says, shaking her head. "I have no idea how you're resisting that hotness. I kind of want to pour my drink on him and lick it off."

Jess pegs Erin with the bottle of tanning lotion she was just using and Erin laughs, the sound echoing off the waves. Jarrett turns toward us and we all snap our mouths shut and face the water again.

"Tell me he did not just see us," Jess whispers. "Oh my God, he's coming over here."

Erin and I are giggling when Jarrett reaches us.

"Jess, can I talk to you?" He frowns, tucking his hands into the pockets of his forest green board shorts. "Please?"

"Is it Wednesday night?"

Jarrett looks confused. "What?"

"If it's not Wednesday night, then I'm not in my Scope and Methods class," Jess asserts, lifting herself from her chair. Even with sunglasses on it's hard for Jarrett to hide the way his eyes are taking in Jess's body now that she's standing. "Therefore, we have nothing to talk about."

"I beg to differ," he starts, but Jess is already halfway to the water.

"See you in class!" she calls out behind her before joining Ashlei. Jarrett sighs, gives Erin and I a slight nod of his head, and then makes his way back up the beach.

"Poor guy," Erin says. Jess and Ashlei are wading waist-deep in the water, but neither of them say a word. They just stare out at the boats passing by in the distance and let the ocean breeze roll through their hair. As Erin drifts off in her chair, I fall into the comfortable silence and my thoughts settle on the one person who seems to haunt them most nowadays.

Adam.

My stomach twinges and I shift in my chair. No matter how much I tell myself I need to stop, I can't quit thinking about our kiss. More specifically – what the kiss was to him as opposed to what it was to me. When his lips met mine, I felt a spark – an electricity I've never experienced before. It caught at the point of contact and spread like wildfire through my entire body within seconds.

But then he pulled back and brushed it off like it was nothing to him.

And maybe it wasn't.

That's what kills me most.

Friends. That's what he wants to be. And now that I know Skyler is interested in him, too, I'm doubly screwed. Is there a protocol for Big/Littles liking the same guy? Do I tell her I like him? Would that be selfish since he essentially said kissing me was weird?

Sighing, I fall deeper into my chair and pull my psychology textbook from my beach bag. Our chapters this week cover the signs and psychology of social acceptance and unrequited love. Though I know what I'm feeling is far from love, the coincidence isn't lost on me.

We stay on the beach until the sun sets and then pack up our bags and head back to campus.

The girls drop me at my dorm on their way to the house and Paris is home when I arrive.

She looks up at me, assesses the beach gear I'm still holding, and then looks back down at the fingernail she's painting. She doesn't even acknowledge me and I can't decide if it pisses me off or just feels like a punch to the gut.

"Hey, Paris."

"Hey."

"Going out tonight?"

"I have a sorority event at the house in an hour."

"Oh," I say softly. "Okay. Well do you maybe want to hang out tomorrow night after your late class?"

"Sorry, can't."

"What about Thursday?"

"Busy."

"Friday?"

She sighs, tightening the lid on the bright pink polish and blowing on her fresh coat. "Honestly, Cassie? I really don't want to hang out. No offense, but I've got a lot going on with Zeta right now and I know you probably do with KKB, too." She wrinkles her nose a bit as she says my letters and I clench my teeth.

"I'm not too busy to hang out with my best friend. Or has that changed and I'm just unaware?"

"We're in college now, Cassie," Paris says, resigned. "Aren't we a little old for the best friends thing?"

Shaking my head, I don't even answer her question before storming back to my room, silently thanking my parents for getting me a dorm with separate bedrooms. I slam the door and toss my beach bag in the corner before falling face first onto my bed. I want to cry, or scream, or anything that will help get the emotion out of me but nothing comes. When my phone's beachy ringtone fills the silence, I reach for it and answer before even checking caller ID.

"Hello?"

"What are you doing?"

I bolt upright when I recognize Adam's voice on the other end of the line. "Just got home from the beach."

"Are you hungry? My class just ended and I'm starved and could use a beer. Want to hit The Plaza with me?"

I swallow. "Uh, sure. What time do you want to meet?"

"I'm heading there now. Just come to Pie Heaven when you're ready."

"Okay. See you in a minute."

I don't even bother changing and within fifteen minutes I'm walking into the pizza place. The Plaza is a casual little shopping center with a few restaurants, two bars, and a dozen little Mom and Pop shops ranging from a nail salon to a custom t-shirt shop. When I walk into Pie Heaven, Adam is already there. He waves at me from a booth in the very back.

"I ordered us a large pepperoni. You're not a vegetarian, are you?"

"Nope. Total meat lover here." My eyes grow wide as the words leave my lips and I realize the implication behind them. *Could I be any more of a spazz?*

Adam smirks. "Good to know. How was the beach?" As his eyes scan my bathing suit and small cover-up I suddenly wish I would have taken the time to change. I can only imagine how my hair looks after being in salt water and wind all day.

"Fun. Coming home, on the other hand…"

"What happened? Roommate drama still?"

"Unfortunately."

Adam crosses his arms across his chest and leans back. "Whatever. Her loss. Zetas are bitches, anyway."

I laugh at that just as the waitress drops off our pizza. Adam immediately digs in, draining the rest of his beer to wash down the first slice which I'm almost positive he just inhaled. There was no chewing going on.

"You going to Ralph's next week for Halloween?"

"I heard that I really don't have a choice," I reply. "Sounds like that's what everyone does."

"It's a huge block party. There are other bars hosting events, but Ralph's is the place to be. It always has been."

"Well, then I guess I'll be there."

"Cool. Me too. Is Skyler going?"

My heart sinks along with my smile. "I'm not sure. She's been really busy training lately."

"Training? For what?"

"She has a poker tournament this weekend."

"Oh shit, I didn't know she played. That girl is full of surprises."

"Yeah."

Adam watches me carefully for a moment before speaking again. "Well, regardless, I'll be there. Do you know what you're dressing up as yet?"

"I'm deciding between Ariel from *The Little Mermaid* and a zombie bride."

Adam quirks a brow. "Those are two very different directions."

"Yeah, well, I haven't decided if I want to be cute and innocent or scary as hell."

He smirks, wiping his mouth with a napkin and finishing his second beer. "Well, my vote is for Ariel."

"Yeah? It's not too cliché?" I twirl a strand of my frizzy, beach-blown hair around my index finger. "You know, red hair and all?"

"Nah," he asserts, watching me with a sideways grin. "Besides, I think you'd be cute in a little purple shell bra."

My cheeks flush, but I don't know if Adam notices as he calls the waitress over for the check. He pays and then walks me back to my dorm, chatting about the concert almost the entire way. Once I'm back in my room, I strip down and run a cold shower. Even with the icey water raining down, my skin is still red hot.

And something tells me it's not a sunburn.

Jess

I'VE NEVER REALLY LOVED SCHOOL, but class feels especially long tonight. It could have something to do with the fact that Jarrett's eyes haven't left me for more than thirty seconds. Every time I glance over at him, he's staring at me – and not in a creepy way, but in the way that makes me feel like he's weighing all the options he has for how to take my clothes off.

It's so strange, seeing him dressed in sharp black slacks and a gray button up shirt with a black vest to match. I'll always see him in board shorts and a t-shirt, just like that first night. Just like yesterday on the beach when I avoided him. That man belongs on a beach – or at least somewhere where he's not restricted by clothes.

When Dr. Maynard releases us and Jarrett finishes calling attendance, I pack up my bag and keep my eyes fixed on the door as I walk past him. When a strong hand wraps around my wrist just as I reach the door, I close my eyes and exhale through my nose.

"We need to talk."

"No, we don't," I say softly, watching the other students pass. None of them notice us, but I'm still paranoid. When the last person leaves and we're the only ones left in the room, Jarrett curses.

"It's been almost two months. Why are you avoiding me?"

I scoff. "Really? If you have to ask, you're seriously stupid."

"It doesn't have to be like this, Jess." His dark eyes are sheltered beneath furrowed brows. "I don't... I didn't want what happened to be a one time thing."

"Yeah, well, it was."

Jarrett blinks. "Is that all you wanted?"

No.

"Obviously. You knew that when you took me in the back of your truck." Saying the words out loud, even though we're alone, makes me blush. And I *never* blush.

Jarrett's mouth thins out into a flat line. "Don't act like you're not still attracted to me. Don't act like you don't watch me every class. Don't act like you don't have the same things going through your mind that I do right now." He steps closer to me, reaching his hand up to grasp behind my neck. My eyelids flutter at the contact but I keep my cool. "You want me. And I want you."

Fuck.

Like seriously, FUCK.

Pulling away, my eyes fall to the floor and I notice his bag is packed with a change of clothes – board shorts included. I need to kill this – whatever *this* is – between us, and I think I know exactly how to do it.

"You're my professor's assistant," I state firmly, though my voice sounds shaky. "The only thing I want from you is the answer key to our next test."

With that, I turn on my heel and push through the heavy wooden door of the classroom.

Then, I set my plan into motion.

MY VAGINA is trying to talk me out of my plan the entire drive to the beach.

What is wrong with you? Fuck him, you idiot!

But it's not that simple. Do I want to keep hooking up with Jarrett? Obviously. The way he pulled my hair and grabbed my neck in the back of that truck has me more than curious about what he could do with an entire bed at his disposal. The sad truth is that he *is* my professor's assistant. He could get fired, I could get expelled, we could both damage our reputations – both professionally and socially.

So tonight, I'll get my point across.

My light cotton spaghetti strap dress sticks to my skin as I walk through the sand to the beach bar. I could blame the still-hot-even-though-it's-October Florida air, but the truth is that I'm nervous. I don't know if what I'm doing is even what I really want. All I know is that it has to happen.

Jarrett's eyes find mine as soon as I walk through the entryway. His hand that was just wiping down the left end of the bar halts and he stares. Swallowing, I walk purposefully up to him and order a beer. As soon as he slides it into my hand, I drop cash on the bar and strut over to a group of guys I recognize from school.

Game time.

One of the guys is Josh, Clinton's little, and he just so happens to be the easiest guy I've ever known. I'm pretty sure he'd hit on a plastic bag if the wind blew it in a way that made it resemble tits. As soon as he sees me, he jumps out of his chair.

"Oh shit! J-Love has graced us with her presence!"

"And you're damn lucky, too."

He swoops me up into a hug and I giggle, though only for show. I am not into Josh in any way, shape, or form. Josh has an amazing upper body, but he's missed one too many leg days and his skin is constantly a burnt orange from the self-tanner he applies daily. His hair is a light brown, but I swear he dyes it. There is no way this kid isn't a ginger. If his freckles aren't a dead giveaway, the brownish-red beard he's sporting right now certainly is.

Josh's brothers order the first round of shots and I make sure to lean into Josh more than necessary, letting his hands rest on my hips and ass. I don't even have to look Jarrett's way to know he's watching. I can practically feel my skin burning.

"Where's Bear tonight?"

"No idea. Probably changing his tampon." My brows shoot up. Josh has always been very respectful to Bear. "He's been a pussy lately. He keeps raggin' on us for partying, saying shit about how we're going to get us in trouble. Plus he's been moody as hell for no damn reason. Don't you remember him freaking out on Skyler at our party a few weeks ago?"

"Oh yeah. That was awkward."

"Yeah. Whatever." He grins with a smile too big for his face and pulls me in closer. "The real question is, what do you want to drink next?"

Ick. Typical Josh. He always has to get a girl wasted before he can get laid, which only makes my skin crawl more at the fact that I have to use him of all guys to get Jarrett off my ass. But he's easy, and he's working. I saunter up to the bar pretending like I'm still giggling about something Josh said and order another round of shots.

Jarrett fills the order silently, slamming glasses around more than necessary. After he pours the blue liquid in a straight line over the shot glasses, he snatches the cash from my hand but holds my gaze.

"What are you doing?"

"Paying for shots," I deadpan. "Should I be doing something else?"

With that, I gather up the shots and make my way back to the table, casting a glance back at Jarrett just to confirm that he's watching my ass.

And he so is.

As the night progresses, Josh pushes his luck more and Jarrett watches every minute of it. I feel kind of shitty using Josh, but I need to piss Jarrett off. I need him to see that I'm not interested, he was just a one night stand, nothing more and nothing less.

Even if it is a lie.

The truth is, I would love nothing more than to take him in his truck again and feel his strong hands splayed on my lower back as I ride his massive cock. But he's my teacher – or, pretty close to it – and he could get fired. For some reason, I care about him enough to not want that.

Which is also weird.

"You're so damn sexy," Josh whispers into the nape of my neck before kissing his way up to my earlobe. He bites it seductively, but I don't feel the slightest bit turned on.

"Can you walk me to my car?" I flirt, biting my lip. I made sure to stop after the first two shots, fake drinking my beer and refilling the guys' drinks as necessary. I fully intend to drive my happy ass home tonight.

Josh groans. "Gladly."

As we stumble toward the door, Josh cups my ass in his hands and I swat at him playfully, letting him kiss up and down my neck. When we reach the entryway, I cast one last glance at Jarrett. His dark eyes are haunting, his jaw tense beneath the skin stretched over it. His nose flares with every breath as he watches Josh push me the last bit out the door, and then he's out of view.

And I'm off the hook.

I keep Josh occupied for a half hour, kissing him feverishly in the back of my BMW. When I think it's been long enough for him to walk back into the bar and raise eyebrows, I peel him off me and open the door.

"Thanks, Josh. See you around."

"Wait, what?" The look on his face almost makes me feel bad.

Almost.

"Yeah, not happening, Josh," I say, crawling into the front seat. The engine purrs to life and Josh slowly crawls out of the back seat, his face still twisted in confusion.

"What the fuck was all that?"

I shrug. "Just having a little fun. Like I said, see you around." I flash him a smile and then pull away, leaving him stroking his ego and maybe something else in the parking lot.

The farther I get away from the bar, the more I feel like I can breathe. I blast Eric Church as loud as I can to drown out whatever thoughts of Jarrett are still stuck in my head, but it only helps momentarily.

It was luck running into Josh tonight. I figured I'd have to work hard for some business suit to walk out the door with me, but I lucked into him and his brothers breaking away from the normal college bars. Jarrett saw everything, he saw that he wasn't anything special, and now I don't have to worry about him trying to seduce me.

Mission accomplished.

Skyler

A HARD KNOCK on my bedroom door wakes me from my nap and I groan. "Go away."

"Sky? It's me..."

My eyes fly open at the sound of Clinton's voice. Snatching my phone from the table, I sigh when I see I haven't even been asleep for twenty minutes. With the news I got from my parents last week coupled with practicing for my upcoming tournament, I haven't been sleeping at night. Afternoon naps are my only savior, and this one just got interrupted.

But Clinton hasn't talked to me since the O Chi party when he blew up on me. I've tried texting him, calling him, showing up at his room – but he's avoided me every time. So, as much as I really want to hit snooze and tell him to go away again, I refrain.

"Come in."

I sit up in my tiny bed and attempt to fix my disheveled hair as he peeks in. Seeing that I'm decent, he lets the door close behind him and stands awkwardly in front if it with his hands in his pockets. "Hey."

"Hi."

I don't know what else to say. Clinton and I have never been in an argument, but I pushed him too hard at the party and he let me know that I needed to back off. It's hard for me to do. Clinton is one of my best friends and I don't know how to help him if he won't tell me what's going on.

Of course, the past week and a half I've been more occupied with my own shit. Dad didn't get the promotion he'd been promised, which means the money he and Mom spent on fixing up the house thinking he'd have the paycheck to pay it off set them back. By a lot. I have a gut feeling there's more they aren't telling me because they don't want me to worry, but it just makes me even more anxious.

I'm entered in a fairly large tournament at the casino downtown on Tuesday. If I win, I could pay off the credit card debt they racked up and finish paying off my tuition from this semester. It's the biggest tournament I've played in a long time. With stakes this high, I've been practicing every night – and it's definitely catching up to me.

Clinton lets out a heavy exhale, breaking me from my thoughts. It's then that I notice how rough he looks. His dark skin is even darker under his eyes and his shoes don't match his hat, which is saying a lot for Clinton. "Look, Skyler. I'm sorry.

I'm bad at this shit but I'm sorry I blew up on you. You didn't deserve it, you were just trying to help and I was a dick."

I shrug, trying not to make a big deal about it. He hurt my feelings, but at the same time I meant what I said to the girls when I said he'd come around when he was ready. That's the way Clinton works. "It's all good, Bear. I'm just worried about you."

"I know you are." His eyebrows knit together as he assesses my appearance. "Shit, by the looks of you maybe it's me who should be worried."

I run my fingers through my tangled hair. "Yeah. Tournament this week."

"Yeah? Been at the casino every night getting in some practice?"

I nod, yawning. "Exactly."

Clinton sits down on the bed next to me and pulls me into his big chest, his arms enveloping me in a warm hug that almost puts me back to sleep. "You stress yourself out too much with this."

"Well, I have a lot to lose. And a lot to gain."

"Family stuff again?"

Clinton doesn't know the whole story with my family. He gets the gist of it – I grew up piss poor and I have to work for everything I want and need

– but he doesn't know that I also have to provide for my family. Or, rather, I choose to.

"Dad didn't get the promotion like he thought he would. Mom said they racked up some credit card debt, but I think it might be more than that, Bear." I lean up to look at him. "I think there's something they're not telling me."

"So you're going to kick everyone's ass at this tournament and then send some money home?" I nod and Clinton smiles. "'Attagirl. Are you going to Ralph's for the annual Halloween rager?"

"I doubt it. That's the day after the tournament. I'll probably sleep through it."

"What?" Bear jumps up, making me instantly miss his warm embrace. "Oh hell no. You need to have some fun, Sky. You're prepared enough. Get some rest and enjoy your college experience."

"It's just one party."

"But it's the *Halloween* party," he points out.

I chuckle, but concede. "Well, when you put it like that." Clinton winks and sits back down on the bed. Without even asking, I lean into him again and let my eyes close.

"We have an intramural football game tomorrow. You should come."

I nod against his chest, but don't have the

energy to say anything else. He chuckles and leans us back, holding me until I succumb to sleep.

I'VE NEVER REALLY BEEN A SPORTS PERSON, other than poker – which is still kind of tough for me to see as a sport. In high school, I was too unpopular to be involved in any sporting events and in college I only go to support the guys. I can't name one professional team of any variety and I have no idea what the penalties mean, but I'm still geared up in green and black – Omega Chi Beta colors – with Cassie as we cheer on Clinton and his brothers against Alpha Sigma.

"I'm glad you came out tonight, Big," Cassie says, smiling. "I feel like you've been hidden away the past two weeks."

"I know, I'm sorry. It's just –"

"The tournament," she interrupts, still smiling. "I know, I know. I'm just glad you're finally hanging out with me."

I frown a little at that, but decide not to think too much about it. I'm here now. That's what matters.

Cassie and I jump off the bench every time O Chi scores, cheering like we should be carrying pompoms. Even though the leaves don't really turn colors in South Florida, being outside cheering on a football game gets me in the fall spirit. When the last whistle is blown, the score is twenty-one to seven – Omega Chi Beta.

Clinton throws me up and over his shoulder when he rushes off the field, spinning me around and cheering. I beat my tiny fists against his back to no avail and end up just giving in, celebrating with him. When he finally puts me down, the grin I'm so accustomed to seeing is plastered on his face. *This* is the Clinton I know, the Clinton I've missed.

"Fuck yeah! You saw me sack that wimpy ass Alpha Sig, right?" Clinton holds up his hand for a high five and I slap mine against it.

"You were awesome, Bear."

"Fuck yeah he was," Josh chimes in. I fight against the urge to roll my eyes as he throws his arm around my shoulder. "You coming out to celebrate with us, Sky?"

"She has to practice for her poker tournament," Cassie chimes in.

"Boo," Josh says, but I'm thankful that he pulls his arm off me and rushes toward his brothers. Clinton gives me one last hug and then joins them.

"Uh oh, I smell trouble," a voice says behind us. Cassie and I turn around at the same time to see Adam.

Shirtless.

"Are you sure that's trouble? Might be defeat."

Adam clutches his bare chest and stumbles back a bit, tossing his drenched red shirt over his shoulder. The view of his insanely cut arms and chest is definitely a nice sight. "Ouch, Skyler. Why don't you just kick a guy while he's down?"

I giggle and bite my lip. Adam is cute. No, he's *hot* – and seeing his dark hair mussed on top of his head right now only makes me think of the last time I saw him that way, after rolling around in my bed for half the afternoon.

"What'd you think of the game?" he asks Cassie. She blushes and I shake my head. My Little is so damn innocent. Just talking to a boy makes her nervous. How the hell did she end up with me as a Big?

"It was good. You were good."

He grins. "Does that mean you'll give me a loser hug?"

Cassie's eyes bulge as she takes in his sweaty body, but he doesn't give her a chance to run before he wraps her in his arms and spins her around. She squeals and flails her legs until he finally puts her down.

"Thanks for the help, Big!"

"Hey, I'm not trying to get up in that sweaty mess."

Adam turns his attention to me. "Oh yeah?" I take off sprinting in the opposite direction but he catches me easily and smothers me against his slick chest. I have to say, I don't really mind it.

"You going to Ralph's Wednesday?" he asks, finally letting me free.

"I'm thinking about it."

"You should go."

"Oh yeah? Why's that?"

"Because I'll be there."

I bite my lower lip and assess him. I can't say for sure, but I think I just might like Adam Brooks. "Well I have a tournament tomorrow night, so I might be too tired to go."

"Oh yeah," he muses. "I heard about you and your kick ass poker skills. Can I come watch?"

"Um, absolutely not."

He blanches. "Why not?"

"I don't really mix business with... pleasure," I say, quirking a brow on the last word. Adam smiles at me devilishly, but doesn't press the subject. Suddenly, his eyes flick behind me and his face hardens. When I turn to see what he's staring at, Cassie is blushing talking to one of Adam's brothers.

"Isn't that your president?"

"Yeah."

Adam is still focused on the scene behind me when I turn back around, his mouth flattened into a thin line. "I take it you don't exactly care for him?"

"That's putting it lightly," he scoffs. "The guy's a dick." He shakes his head and turns his attention back to me. "Let me come to the tournament with you."

"Not a chance."

Adam narrows his eyes. "Fine. Well, at least tell me what you'll be dressed as at Ralph's so I can find you. Because let's be honest, you'll be there. Everyone will be there."

I roll my eyes, but can't really argue with him. "Are you going to dress as the other half of my costume if I tell you what it is?"

"Maybe."

"Well then, I'll either be Sandy from Grease, the black swan, or a princess. Choose your costume wisely."

With that, I throw him a wink and saunter back over to Cassie before linking my arm in hers and pulling her away from Adam's president, who she informs me is named Clay. When I cast a glance back, Adam is still staring, shaking his head with his arms crossed over his chest.

Maybe this party won't be so bad after all.

Cassie

I LEARN QUICKLY that Halloween in a sorority house is an explosion of glitter, spandex, and makeup.

Adjusting my boobs in the too-small purple shell top the girls talked me into, I look around at all the costumes. Bo is a sexy ninja and Ashlei is a go-go dancer. They're both giggling in the corner of Skyler and Jess's room as they apply the last of their fake eyelashes in the full length mirror. Bo's outfit is a two-piece and hugs her tight body, accentuating the lean muscle that stretches all the way from her collarbone to her ankles. Ashlei's neon green dress cuts off just below her ass, but it pairs well with the white go-go boots that end at the top of her knee caps. It feels good to see Ashlei laughing again. She's been distant the past two weeks and I know I'm not the only one who's been worried.

"Are you sure I look okay?" I ask, picking at the sequin green skirt hugging my waistline. "I feel a little cliché going as the only redheaded princess."

"You look fucking hot," Jess says, smacking my ass as she saunters over to her closet. She's dressed as a sexy cowgirl, complete with a tight, short jean skirt and plaid top that ties off right beneath her chest. Her cleavage is accentuated by the open buttons at the top of the shirt and she tops it all off with a straw cowgirl hat and matching brown boots.

"She's right, Little. Just watch out for nip slips." Skyler winks and pops her lips after applying a final coat of lip gloss. Of all the costumes, I love Skyler's the most. She's the only one of us who didn't openly go for sexy but landed there anyway. Dressed as the black swan complete with black spandex one-piece and tutu, she's not just sexy – she's intriguing. In fact, she's almost scary – especially with the contacts she's wearing that color her eyes red just like Natalie Portman's in the movie.

When Erin blows the whistle that came with her bedroom referee costume, we all jump. "Let's get the hell out of here. I need a drink!"

We all cheer before following her through the house and out into the yard. Several cabs are lined up and down Greek row waiting to pick up fares, so we climb in the first van we see and the cabbie takes off without even asking where to.

"You look great tonight," Ashlei says to Bo quietly. The three of us are sandwiched in the very back of the van and I adjust our air conditioning vents, trying to keep my hair from frizzing out in the hot October air. I swear it never gets cold in South Florida.

"Thanks," Bo replies, offering Jess a glittering smile. Her hand reaches out for Ashlei's knee and she squeezes it lightly. "Although, I think we both know I look a little more than just great."

She says the last part as a whisper, but I still hear her, and I can't help but notice she doesn't move her hand from Ashlei's leg. I don't have time to overthink it as Skyler thrusts a flask into my hand. "Drink up, Little Nug."

Ralph's is always packed, being that it's the closest bar to campus, but tonight it's on an entirely new level. The entire parking lot is sealed off by a makeshift fence for the block party and there are laser lights bouncing in time with the music thumping from the large speakers by the entrance to the main bar. Fog machines, cobwebs, mechanical monsters and mummies bring the Halloween theme to life and I finally understand what all the fuss is about.

Jess, Ashlei and Bo immediately sprint to the makeshift dance floor and start grinding on each other and every guy around them while Erin scampers off to find the rest of our family. Skyler and I just make a beeline for the bar.

Priorities.

Just as we down a lemon drop shot and chase it with our fresh drinks, large hands wrap around my waist. "I was right." The butterflies that have been lying dormant in my stomach since the IM football game Monday night suddenly burst to life and flutter around manically. Adam sidles up beside me, one of his hands still lingering on my hip as he throws me a wide smile. "You do look cute in a little purple shell bra."

He looks absolutely delicious. His dark hair is gelled in a 50s style twist and black-framed Ray Bans hide his eyes but accentuate his strong jaw. The white shirt he's wearing blazes against his tan skin and stretches across his hard chest muscles. Paired with a black leather jacket and tight dark jeans, he's the entire Danny Zuko package and I imagine him giving young John Travolta a run for his money.

"Almost as cute as you in your little leather jacket," I retort, cringing once the words leave my lips. *Really? Did I really just call him cute?*

Adam just grins wider.

Suddenly, Skyler bursts into a fit of laughter and both of our heads snap in her direction. "I'm sorry," she says, trying to control herself.

I'm still confused but Adam seems to catch on to the joke because he lets out a loud spurt of laughter, too. "Well shit. I guess I picked the wrong costume, huh?"

Skyler nods. "Yeah. I mean, unless we're doing a really terrifying mashup of Black Swan and Grease."

Adam grabs his chin between his finger and thumb and looks up at the ceiling. "You know, that might not be half bad."

Clearly, I missed out on the joke.

"Dance with me?" Skyler asks, but it doesn't really sound like much of a question as she grabs Adam's hand and leads him toward where Jess and Bo are still dancing wildly. As soon as they reach the floor, Skyler runs her hands up through Adam's hair and grinds her body against his. He bites his lip and pushes his sunglasses up onto the top of his head so he has a better view and my stomach flutters again, but in a completely different way.

Quickly, I drain the rest of my drink and order another one.

"Hey you." Clay appears right behind me and wraps his arms around my middle, pulling me flush against his chest. It's a bold move for having only met me a couple of days ago. "I can't find room at this damn bar. Order me a drink?" he whispers.

I peek over my shoulder at him. "What's your drink of choice?"

"Hmm..." he thinks, still holding me tight. "How about whiskey on the rocks. That always gets me in the mood." I gulp at his suggestion, but he just chuckles in my ear. "To party, that is."

I smile nervously and order his drink before turning to face him. His hands stay on my hips as I swivel around. When I notice he's dressed as a lifeguard, I swallow. His abs are on full display. Every single freaking *ripple* of his body is on display, actually, in the tiny red board shorts he's donning. His dirty blonde hair is wavy and messy and the bright blue hues of his eyes contrast with the bronzer he's clearly applied to pull off the beachy look. I didn't realize how tall he was on the field Monday, but the way he's towering over me now makes me feel six inches tall.

The corners of his mouth curl into a devilish grin as my eyes wander across his skin. "You think a mermaid could dance with a lifeguard?" he asks, quirking a brow.

"Well, I did pass over the part where I have a tail and skipped straight to the legs."

"And what incredible legs they are," he husks, allowing his own eyes to devour my body now. Clay grabs my hand and pulls me out onto the dance floor before I have the chance to say anything further. As I turn away from him and we grind our bodies to the beat, I catch Adam staring at me from where Skyler and the girls are gathered. His brows are furrowed, his mouth pursed, and he looks like he wants to either kill me or save me.

Suddenly, the butterflies are back.

Jess

"I HAVE TO PEE," I slur, finishing my drink before slamming the plastic cup on the bar. "Be right back."

"Want me to go with you?" Ashlei asks, her eyes wide at the thought of me going to the bathroom by myself.

I giggle. "I'm fine, Lei. Keep my Little company and order me a shot. Be back in a sec."

Ashlei's eyes find Bo's and she smiles. "I can do that."

The bathroom is packed with girls just as drunk as me waiting to pee. I pull a bitch move and tell them I'm just going to use the mirror as I pass until I duck inside the first empty stall that opens up. After I relieve myself, I really do check my reflection and thank sweet baby Jesus for the waterproof makeup Ashlei let me use. My eyes still look awesome and after a quick touch up of gloss, I'm ready to go.

Another text message from Josh comes through my phone as I make my way back to the bar and I sigh. The kid just can*not* take a hint.

Suddenly, I'm ripped backward and my phone flies out of my hand and crashes to the floor, splintering in three different directions. I panic as a hand is crushed over my mouth and I'm yanked back into a dark, confined closet.

"I would tell you not to scream, but that defeats the purpose of this," a deep voice growls in my ear. I recognize it immediately.

Jarrett.

He removes his hand from my mouth and I gasp, my heart still beating rapidly in my chest. His hands move to my hips and he pulls my back against his chest, his breath hot in my ear. "You think those little boys you're toying with can give you what you want?" His voice is husky, dark, and laced with desire. Instantly, my panties grow wet and I moan as he nips at the skin on my neck. "I think you've forgotten what I can do to you, Jess – what I can make you *feel*. I'm here to remind you."

With that, he whips me around and his mouth crashes down on mine. His kiss is passionate and needy. He discards my cowgirl hat before fisting his hands in my hair as my nails rake his back. I know I should push him away, I should remind *him* that he could get fired for this. But right now, the alcohol swimming in my system paired with the intense way Jarrett's tongue is moving against mine is crippling my desire to make him stop.

I *definitely* do not want him to stop.

Jarrett grabs both of my thighs in his hands and lifts me, crashing us back against a shelf. I still can't see anything but I feel product crash all around us as I wrap my legs tight around his waist, using the leather from my cowgirl boots to gain traction and hold my ankles together.

"You walk into class every Wednesday night," he pants against my skin, letting his hand trail down my neck. I moan when his fingertips dip inside the low-cut v-line of my shirt and graze my nipple. "Looking sexy as fuck," he continues, his hand sliding up under my jean skirt. "And you just ignore me." His fingers rub slow circles on the fabric of my lace panties and I buck against his touch. "You *torture* me." He slips one finger inside the lace and rubs my opening. "Christ, you're so wet, Jess. You're so ready for me. Why do you pretend like you don't want me?"

"I do want you," I whisper, kissing him again. The music from the bar is muffled inside the closet and every breath shared between us is amplified.

"Are you sure?" he teases, sliding the tips of his two fingers against my core as his other hand works to hold me pinned against the wall. I squirm, rotating my hips to try to get his fingers where I really want them.

"It's dangerous."

"Maybe," he agrees, his fingers stilling. He pauses for a moment and I think maybe he might be realizing what could happen if we get caught. Then suddenly, he slides his fingers inside me in one smooth thrust and kisses me hard, pulling my bottom lip between his teeth. "But it's also really fucking fun."

My moans turn to screams as his fingers work inside me. My skirt is now completely bunched at my waist and my hands slide down Jarrett's abdomen until I feel him through his shorts. He's just as ready for me as I was for him and I grip him tightly through the fabric.

"Fuck," he growls, removing his fingers and making quick work of the tie on his shorts. He doesn't wait for me to ask, he just drops my feet to the ground, spins me around so my hands are on the wall, moves my panties to the side and thrusts into me from behind, making me cry out in a mix of pleasure and pain.

His hands move around to palm my breasts as he pumps into me. Each thrust makes me moan more as I feel him growing harder inside me. When he wraps one hand around my neck and uses the other to push me flush against the wall, I let out another cry.

"Do your frat boyfriends fuck you like this?" he husks in my ear, sliding one hand down and around my hips until he finds my clit. My face is pushed hard against the concrete wall and Jarrett uses his free hand to pin mine above my head. "Do they?"

"No," I pant.

"What was that?"

"No!" I scream louder.

"Does anyone fuck you the way I do?"

"No," I whisper again.

Jarrett pounds into me hard, reaching me deeper than ever before. I bite my lip and gasp against the shocking pain mixed with the pleasure still rocking my entire body.

"I'm sorry?"

"No! No one fucks me the way you do!" I scream, not caring if anyone hears at this point. He growls and begins circling my clit wildly, still holding my wrists above my head with his other hand. "I love the way you fuck me, Jarrett," I pant against the concrete. He bites and sucks at the back of my neck in response. "Don't stop, Jarrett. Don't you fucking stop."

"Quitting isn't in my vocabulary, princess."

The combination of his words, his finger working my clit, and his cock thrusting into the deepest parts of my core are too much. The pressure builds until I'm sure I'll combust before I finally tumble over the edge, screaming and moaning Jarrett's name as each wave of pleasure rocks through me. Jarrett curses as he releases too, his entire body convulsing behind me. Our breathing slows and Jarrett moves his hands to grip my hips firmly as he plants kisses down the back of my neck and across my shoulder.

After a moment, as our breathing is still steadying, Jarrett releases me and quickly pulls his shorts back on. My eyes are finally adjusted to the dark, but even so I can barely make out his form. He pushes me back against the wall once more after he dresses, his tongue demanding my own.

"Don't ever fuck around with another guy in front of me," he commands. "It doesn't piss me off, it doesn't make me hate you – it only makes me want you more."

With that, his lips leave mine and he slips out of the closet, leaving me alone in the darkness. My breaths are still ragged, my thong soaked, and my hair a tangled mess as I try to make sense of what just happened.

Holy. Shit.

Cassie

MY MERMAID BRAID is sticking to my neck as I fan myself at the bar waiting for my order to be filled. The night has surprisingly cooled down, but dancing with Clay has done nothing but heat me up.

Clay is definitely good looking, but I've come to realize that there aren't many guys at Palm South who aren't. Besides his looks, I haven't really connected with him on anything, but he's a good time. Tonight, he's a good distraction from other people… people I need to stop thinking about.

"Water?" Adam asks, sliding up beside me at the bar. The way his skin is glistening lets me know he's been dancing just as hard as me.

"It feels like I'm out there doing cardio. I need rehydration."

"Nah, just take another shot. You'll feel better." He smirks, but it fades quickly. "What are you doing with Clay?"

"What do you mean?"

"I mean, are you here with him?"

My stomach twinges at his question, or rather, what the underlying implications of it might be. "No. I don't know. We met the other day at your game and he showed up tonight, so we've been dancing."

"Cassie," he breathes my name, shaking his head slightly. "Don't get caught up with him. He's a dick."

I gulp. "I think he seems nice."

"That's just the thing. He *seems* nice, but I know who he is. He's bad news."

Suddenly, I realize what's going on. Adam is clearly into Skyler, he's shoved me in the friend zone, yet for whatever twisted reason, he doesn't want to see me with someone else. What, does he think I should just wait around long enough for him to have his fun with Skyler and then move on to me?

Yeah. Not happening.

"Well, I think I'm a pretty good judge of character," I state matter-of-factly, trading my water for the fruity cocktail just placed in front of me. "And I can take care of myself. But thanks."

Adam grabs my hand and his brows pull together, worry evident in his features. "Please, Cassie. Just be careful."

"Hey Brooks," Clay says, appearing seemingly out of nowhere and clapping Adam hard on the back. Adam drops my hand and glares at Clay. "Having fun?"

"Yep." The word pops at the end, but his eyes soften as they turn to me once more. "See you around, Cassie."

"Yeah. See you."

Adam rejoins Skyler on the dance floor and they're back to grinding without missing a beat. Clay pulls me in closer, his lips falling to my ear. "Want to get out of here?"

I gulp. I didn't plan on leaving with anyone other than the girls tonight, but part of me wants to prove a point to Adam. He's not going to play me or my Big. If he wants her, which clearly he does, then he needs to focus on her. He needs to know that if we're just friends, the way he declared we were, then he would have to see me with other guys.

I can't believe I'm being so bold. This is definitely a far reach from who I was just a few short months ago. Smiling, I nod to Clay and his grin widens. He laces his fingers with mine and tugs me through the crowd.

As we reach the exit, I glance over my shoulder and find Adam watching me, too. He's scowling and even though Skyler is still pressing her body in all the right places against him, his stare doesn't leave me. I think this is the way a man looks when he realizes he doesn't have it all figured out the way he thought he did.

And that's the thing about Halloween. Everyone feels like they can hide behind a mask or a costume, but in the morning, they still wake up as the person *beneath* the mask. I didn't think Adam was the kind of guy to want to play the game between two sisters, but maybe I don't know him as well as I thought.

With that realization and with his eyes still locked on mine, I smile, wave, and walk through the door.

Skyler

JESS IS UNUSUALLY QUIET as we strip off our sweaty costumes and throw them on our bedroom floor. She keeps alternating between a goofy smile and a twisted look of confusion.

"Are you going to tell me what's going on in that blonde head of yours?"

Jess startles at my words as if I'm pulling her back to reality. "What?"

I quirk a brow. "Care to explain why you're blushing with only me in the room?"

Jess's cheeks shade deeper but she just jumps up into her bed, pulling the sheets up high. "I'm not blushing. I'm still hot from dancing."

I eye her warily, but don't push it. "And yet you're climbing into your clean bed?"

"I'll shower in the morning."

"Okay," I say, chuckling. My phone buzzes and I'm surprised when I see my dad's picture light up the screen. Excusing myself to the bathroom, I answer.

"Hey Pops. A little past your bedtime isn't it?"

"You're on the news!"

My stomach drops. "What?"

"Well, okay, not exactly the news – but a big blog wrote an article and you're featured in it!"

"What are you talking about?"

"Check your email."

Just as he says the words, my phone pings in my ear and I pull it away long enough to pull up the new email from Dad. Sure enough, it links to an article from a large poker blog about the top five hottest women in poker.

And I'm number three.

"Whoa," is all I can say as I read through the small amount of verbiage under my picture. It talks briefly about the tournaments I've won in the past before complimenting me for my most recent win – the tournament Tuesday night. The rest talks about how "smoking hot" I look even in a hoodie and glasses, which makes me roll my eyes.

"Can you believe it?" Dad asks, still excited.

"I mean, it's just an article talking about how attractive I am. I don't know how to feel about it."

Dad scoffs. "Look past that, Sky. The fact that they even know who you are is huge." He pauses and I can almost feel him smiling through the phone. "You're really doing it, girl. You're making it."

I read over the article again. "It is kind of cool, isn't it?"

"Hell yes!" Dad beams. "That's my girl. I'm so proud of you. And just wait, they won't be talking about your looks for long once they realize just how good you are at the game."

"We'll see, Dad."

There's another pause before he speaks again. "Thank you, Skyler. Thank you for sending that money… and for always looking out for us." I feel the worry radiate off him and permeate through the phone. "We should be the ones taking care of you."

"Stop," I say, not allowing him to continue. "You always *have* taken care of me. It's okay to let me help out a little now." I smile, thinking of how my parents were the only real friends I had up until Palm South. "Besides, you're going to get that promotion soon and then you can take me out to dinner."

"It's a date, baby girl."

"I love you, Dad. Night."

"Night."

I thumb through the article once more, sizing up the other girls mentioned. I've heard of every single one of them and the fact that my name is even in the same list as them floors me. Suddenly, my phone buzzes again.

Adam.

"Miss me already?" I ask playfully.

"Actually, yes. Plus, I realized we need to celebrate you winning that tournament Tuesday night."

"Um, didn't we kind of already do that tonight?"

"I suppose, but the night is still young, right?"

I glance at the clock and laugh when I see it's just past three in the morning. "Uh…"

"Just go with it. Come downstairs."

With that, the line goes dead and I'm left shaking my head. Adam Brooks is something else.

I pull on a pair of gym shorts and a PSU tank top before sneaking down the stairs and outside. Adam has changed out of his costume and into a relaxed pair of basketball shorts and t-shirt, yet he still looks just as yummy as he did earlier. Leaning against the pillar of our house, his bright smile is illuminated by the moon and his eyes sparkle as he watches me approach.

"Ever gone banner diving before?" he asks.

"Uh… can't say that I have."

"Well, there's a first for everything."

Every house on Greek row has at least two posts where "banners", AKA bed sheets with text and images on them, hang. Usually, the banners advertise an upcoming event or wish a sister or brother a happy birthday. When Adam explains to me that we're going to be diving into them and tearing them down, I pull back.

"What? We can't do that!" I whisper, as if anyone on the completely empty street would hear me. "That's... vandalism. Or something."

He chuckles, his dark eyes still shining in the moonlight. "I didn't peg you for a good girl."

I purse my lips. "I'm just saying. It's rude."

"Kind of. But wouldn't you love to see the look on the Zetas' faces when they see their precious banner shredded in half?" He's got a point there, I really don't like the Zetas. And what the hell? It's just sheets, not like we're throwing bricks at car windows or anything.

"Screw it," I say and then I take off running down the street and dive straight into one of the Zeta banners proclaiming that their sister should be the Alpha Sig Sweetheart. Adam tries to quiet his laughter as I bounce back off the sheet instead of tearing through it like I'd imagined. My laughter, on the other hand, is incredibly loud and awkward.

When a light flickers on downstairs in the Zeta house, Adam and I both snap our necks in that direction.

"Oh shit," I say, scrambling to pull myself up. Adam pokes fun at me trying to hobble away before he scoops me up in his arms and conceals us behind tall scrub bushes near the edge of their yard.

The Zeta house mom appears on the front porch, straining her neck to look both ways before shrugging and retreating back inside the house. Adam and I both die in a fit of laughter and then I realize how close we are. His arms are still wrapped around me, our mouths are just inches apart.

Adam lifts his fingers to cradle my chin before pulling me in for a long, soft kiss. It's the kind of kiss that doesn't make me want to go jump in the sack, but rather cuddle up to watch a movie. It's sweet.

It's nice.

We spend the rest of the night doing absolutely nothing yet talking about everything. We walk all around campus, get into places we're not supposed to, and even play ding-dong-ditch at a few of the dorm rooms. When the sun starts rising, he drops me back off at the house with another long kiss and then I fall into bed completely exhausted, but happy nonetheless.

Maybe Adam Brooks *isn't* just a fun hookup.

Maybe.

Episode 5

WHAT'S WITH ALL THE FUCKING SECRETS AROUND HERE?!

Jess

"SEE! YOU'VE GOT IT," Cassie encourages right as I lean back too far and bust my ass. The longboard jets out from under my feet and races down the sidewalk as Cassie cringes. "Well, you're getting there."

"I don't think falling eight times within one hour means I'm getting there," I volley, wincing as I lift my sore ass off the concrete. I chase down my board as Cassie rides smoothly beside me, like it's the easiest thing in the world.

"It just takes time. You'll get it." She hops off her board and stomps her foot on the back end, popping it up and tucking it under her arm. As we walk, I continue rubbing my ass. I was serious during rush when I told Cassie I wanted her to teach me how to ride, but I didn't think it would be this difficult. Then again, I've never really been active in any capacity other than catching cycling and Zumba classes at the gym, so it doesn't really make sense that I thought I'd be a natural. I guess I just thought my experience riding other people – er, *things* – would come in handy.

"So, you excited about your first semi-formal?" I ask Cassie as we walk. The sun is fading over the campus, casting it in a soft orange glow. Her hair looks even redder in this kind of light and my appreciation for it grows with every passing minute. I feel like there are too many blondes in the world. I'd love to be a redhead – to stand out the way she does.

"Yeah, but I don't really know what to wear."

"It's kind of like high school. Remember how you got kind of dressed up for homecoming, but *really* decked out for prom? Well, semi-formal is homecoming, formal is prom. Just get a short, sexy dress and do something nice with your hair and makeup."

Cassie sighs. "I need to go shopping."

"Oh! I want in. Let's get the girls to go later this week."

"Deal. Speaking of which, who are you bringing with you?"

My stomach drops at her question, which doesn't make any sense because it's an easy enough one that I already have the answer to, but for some reason my mind immediately snaps to Jarrett. "I think I'm taking Matt."

"The O Chi president?" I nod. "Well, looks like we can be twinzies."

"Wait." I halt, grabbing Cassie's arm. "Are you taking Clay? Holy shit. You like him, don't you?"

Cassie's face screws up. "I don't know. Maybe. He's nice."

"Nice enough to take you home and bang the shit out of you on Halloween?" I waggle my brows and Cassie's face turns crimson red.

"Uh, no. I mean, I went home with him for a while but... we didn't... do... *it*."

"Oh? What *did* you do?"

Cassie covers her face with her hands and starts walking again.

"Oh my God! Spill!" I jog to catch up with her and she mumbles something into her hands, but I can't make it out. "What was that?"

"He went down on me." She says the words just above a whisper even though we're the only ones on this path.

"He ate you out?" I say louder. "Well damn, get it, Cassie!" She shushes me and I just laugh. "You should be proud. Why are you acting like it's a bad thing?"

"I didn't really like it, to be honest. And I think he expected… more."

"Ugh," I groan. "I hate when they don't know what they're doing down there. It's like, why even make the effort if you're just going to slobber and make a mess without getting me off?" Cassie blushes and looks down at the ground, which makes me laugh. "Sorry. I'm kind of crass, aren't I?"

"I'm just not very experienced in this kind of stuff."

I pat her shoulder with sympathy, leaning in a bit. "It just takes time. You'll get there," I tease, repeating her encouragement about me on the longboard. She smacks at my arm but misses as I drop my board and hop on it, speeding down the sidewalk.

"How's my carving?" I call out behind me, my eyes on my feet as I shift my balance from my toes to my heels. Cassie yells something back at me but

I don't hear it. My speed is picking up faster than I anticipated and I realize I'm on a hill. Before I have the chance to jump off or correct it, I slam hard into what feels like a brick wall and bounce back off the board, crashing to the ground.

I groan, squeezing my eyes shut against the pain already throbbing in my skull. When I finally lean up on the heels of my hands and squint to see what I hit, I immediately regret it.

"Well, fuck."

Jarrett reaches down and helps me to my feet, steadying me as I try to gain my balance again. Just having his hands on my arms sends flashbacks of Halloween parading through my memory and suddenly it's not just the fall that's making me feel disoriented.

"Are you okay?"

"Peachy," I remark, snatching my board from the ground. The quick motion of bending over and standing upright again sends me spinning and Jarrett's hands find my waist to steady me again. "My phone on the other hand, not so much."

At that, Jarrett's lips twitch into a devilish smirk. "It was a necessary casualty."

My heartbeat quickens and my mouth feels like I swallowed cotton. I know Jarrett can sense it. He feels my nerves. He can feel me trembling. I know, because he's smirking wider now, his dark eyes hooded in a mixture of lust and amusement. When he bites his lower lip and drags his teeth along the tender flesh, my eyes flutter closed before I realize what I'm doing.

"I can buy you a replacement, if you'd like," he adds, but he says it huskily and I know it's on purpose. "We could go to the mobile store on campus after class Wednesday."

"It's fine," I say, snapping out of my trance. "It's already being fixed." Why is my voice shaking? Why am I staring at him like he's stark ass naked instead of fully clothed in a tight gray t-shirt and basketball shorts? *Wait… he's wearing basketball shorts?* My eyes fall lower and I can clearly see the outline of him straining beneath them.

Oh, for fuck's sake.

Really? Like *really*?

Jarrett coughs and my eyes snap to his. He's clearly entertained by my squirming, one brow quirked as he nonverbally calls me out on my crotch staring.

Clearing my throat, I salute him. "Okay. See you in class." When I turn around and race back toward where Cassie stands watching, I cringe and shake my head. *Did I just salute him? Like a fucking skipper or a sergeant?* Good God, I'm a fucking idiot.

"Was that – "

"Yep. Let's go." I grab Cassie by the crook of her arm and drag her in the opposite direction, regardless of if it was where we were originally heading. When I glance over my shoulder, Jarrett is still watching, his arms crossed over his chest and a smug look cemented on his face. He knows he has the upper hand now. He knows he affects me in a way I can't control.

Fuck me.

Ashlei

I FEEL BETTER TODAY than I have in weeks. It's been rough at the studio, but today I feel strong – focused – and as I spin fast around the pole, the smile on my face is irreplaceable. The moves I've been working on since July are starting to come effortlessly to me and I know if I stay on track, I have a chance of taking the title in January.

That's my sole focus now.

Sometimes it takes getting to a low place, maybe even falling to the bottom, before you realize that it's time to start climbing up again. For me, I didn't know I was falling until I came face to face with the dirt. *Literally.* In a way, I'm glad it happened quickly. At least now I can save myself before it's too late.

A stream of sunlight interrupts the darkness of Kitty Heels as Hayden and Kya enter through the front door. When Hayden's eyes find mine, he offers me a forced smile, but I just drop to the floor and walk in the opposite direction toward the water fountain.

"Hey," he says softly, sliding up next to me as I continue to drink. I wipe my mouth with my wrist when I stand to face him, but the pit in my stomach almost makes me spew the liquid out.

"What do you want, Hayden?"

"Listen, I'm sorry about what happened." He can't even say it out loud, which just makes it hurt more. "We got a little carried away, it happens sometimes when you're high. But it won't happen again."

"Damn right it won't because I'm never touching that shit again. Ever. Do you hear me?" I turn on my heel and retreat back to my pole, but Hayden follows.

"Christ, Ashlei, just wait a second." His long hair is disheveled and stringy, his eyes surrounded by dark circles. Hayden is insanely sexy to me – or at least, he always has been before now – but today he just looks sad. And broken. And pathetic.

He nervously plays with his eyebrow ring as he tries to find the words to say next. "You weren't hurt, right? I mean, everything is okay, right?"

My mouth drops open. "Are you fucking serious?" When he doesn't blanch, I snap my mouth shut. "Wow. You are." Hayden snatches my arm as I try to turn away from him again, but I rip it free.

"Why are you acting so crazy?"

"Crazy?!" I scream louder than I intended. "You shoved me out of a moving vehicle, you vapid asshole. You could have *killed* me."

"We weren't even going thirty miles an hour, Ashlei. It was a joke."

"Yeah, well I'm not laughing."

"We were high."

"Exactly!" I cut him off just as he says the word. "We were being stupid. And you? You're *always* being stupid. You mess around with that stuff like it's not going to catch up with you. Well, I'm done. I've sat on it for weeks now, trying to figure out how I felt about all of it, and now I know. I'm staying to dance, to work for Leslie, but I want no part of what you and Kya are mixed up in. Do you hear me? None."

"Ashlei."

"Eat a wiener, Hayden."

I don't give him the opportunity to answer before I climb back up my pole and start working on my advanced moves, the adrenaline still pumping hard through my veins. There's an achingly heavy pressure on my chest at the thought of not having Hayden in my life anymore, but I know this is the right move. I was crazy to let him talk me into trying cocaine in the first place. I should have known it would blow up in my face.

The night after initiation, I blew off my sisters to hang out with him and Kya. It was only my third time getting high with him, but apparently the third time is a charm. What started as a fun evening letting loose ended up with me limping on the backroads back to campus. Since then, I haven't been myself. I've been lost. The only night I felt even semi-normal was on Halloween with Bo.

I bite my lip at the thought of her and slip a little in my transition, making me fall into a Nose Breaker Drop without meaning to. I catch myself just in time, my face inches from the ground. Circling the pole a few times to gain my composure again, I swing my way back up and do a few rounds, trying to ignore the voice in the back of my mind that wants to talk more about what Bo means to me.

"You okay?" Leslie's voice is kind and soft, but it startles me nonetheless and I drop back to the ground, panting.

"I'm good."

She assesses me for a moment before nodding. "Okay then. I need you sharp for January. I know the holidays are coming up and you're probably stressed with school, but I need your focus here as much as it can be. Can you do that?" I nod. "Great." Her eyes soften and she glances up at

Hayden before addressing me again. "I'm always here if you need help, Ashlei." She levels her eyes and I have a feeling she means more than just pole practice, but I just give a curt nod again and climb back on the pole.

I need to work out this adrenaline – and fast. When I go back to the house, it's shopping and semi-formal preparation. How I ended up in two vastly different worlds, I'll never know – but balancing them is getting to be more of a challenge than what I thought I signed up for.

Adam

"GOD, YOU TASTE SO GOOD," I moan into Skyler's neck, trailing my tongue across her skin. She moans and I grind between her legs harder, pulling the sheets up and over our heads. The movie we put on almost two hours ago is now playing the credits, but it doesn't matter because we haven't seen a single minute of it.

"Best Friday night ever," she whispers before leaning up to press her mouth to mine. She bites my bottom lip between her teeth and holds it there as I continue building the friction between us. If we don't actually fuck soon, I might bust in my basketball shorts.

Lifting one of her legs to rest on my shoulder, I slide her wet panties to the side and thrust my fingers inside. Each time I've fingered her tonight, I've brought her just to the edge of pleasure before pulling out and teasing her more. She's been doing the same to me, working us both up to the point where I don't think we'll last more than two minutes once we actually take our clothes off.

"Fuck," Skyler groans. "I can't take this anymore. Take your shorts off."

"Wait," I demand, still teasing her. Her eyes pop open and she glares at me.

"Don't make me ask you again." She smirks, but the undertone of her voice lets me know she's serious. Her delicate fingers shove my shorts down over my ass and she grips me tight, pumping as she maneuvers out of her underwear. When I finally rip open a condom and slide inside her, I know my theory about time is correct.

"Oh God," she moans after just a few thrusts. "I can't hold out, Adam."

"Don't," is all I manage before we both come, our bodies trembling together at the release we've been working toward for hours. When we're finally spent, I roll over to lie beside her, panting. She giggles and curls into my chest and I tuck my arm under her shoulder, pulling her closer.

"Seriously though, best way to spend Friday night."

"No arguments here," I say, kissing her hair. Gently, I run my fingertips up and down her arm, lulling her into a post-orgasm trance. As the music from the movie credits fills the room along with our steady breathing, I pull Skyler in closer and nuzzle my nose into her neck. She sighs contently and holds me in response.

Ever since Halloween, Skyler and I have been pretty much inseparable. Whenever I'm not tied up with fraternity events and she's not playing poker, we're together. She turns me on no matter what she's doing, and apparently she feels the same about me because we hardly spend time outside of the bedroom. I'm not complaining about it, either – not even a little bit. I haven't had a steady hookup in over a year. It's kind of nice to know I can call her at pretty much anytime and she'll be here.

"Hey," I say softly, still trailing my fingertips across her skin. "How's the other half of the slip-n-slide sisters doing?"

"Mmm?" Skyler asks, still dazed.

"Your Little?"

"She's good," Skyler responds sleepily. "Her roommate is a bitch, but nothing new there."

"They're still having problems?"

Skyler nods against my chest. "Yeah. Cassie has been pretty down about it lately. Apparently Paris said some hurtful things to her last weekend." Skyler leans up, kissing me quickly. "I hate to say this, but I have to go."

"You should stay," I try, pulling her back down to the bed. She giggles, but evades my grip and hops out of bed, jumping into her tight jeans. The view is quite nice.

"I don't sex and stay, Adam Brooks."

I frown. "Ouch. I figured we were a little different than your… usual."

At that, she smiles and leans in for another long kiss. "We are. I think. But I can't be sure yet."

"Fair enough." God knows I can't expect her to commit when I know I'm not ready for that, either. "Text me tomorrow."

"You got it, stud." Skyler throws me a wink before climbing out of my bedroom window. She could have gone through the house to the front door, but odds are there are still guys partying in the living room, and I'm betting Skyler doesn't want to answer to all that.

When I hear Clay's annoying ass laugh filter back through the hallway, I roll my eyes, but then my thoughts instantly land on Cassie. Snagging my phone off the bedside table, I type out a quick text.

- You busy tomorrow? -

It's the first thing I've said to Cassie since our confrontation on Halloween, if that's even what that was. I'm not sure. I feel like maybe I should be apologizing to her, but I can't really figure out what for. I meant what I said when I told her Clay was bad news. From what I've heard, she's still been hanging out with him. As much as I want to support whatever choice she makes in regards to who she hooks up with, I can't co-sign anything that has to do with Clay.

I'm a little surprised when she answers a minute later.

- Going shopping with the girls for semi-formal. -

- Breakfast with me first? -

A few minutes pass before she responds.

- Sure. Café? -

- See you at 10. -

I set an alarm on my phone and fall back against my bed, stretching out and working my muscles still sore from the tension of tonight's festivities. When I roll over on my stomach and shove my arm under the pillow, I feel a piece of paper crumble beneath the weight of my hand. Retrieving it, I smile at the note from Skyler with a silly face and an inside joke.

Skyler Thorne is not a one-guy kind of gal. I didn't know that when I met her, but I've figured it out along the way. I'm not saying I'm ready to be in a relationship, either – but at the same time, I really like Skyler. She's fun, feisty, and different. We spend all of our free time together and, to my knowledge at least, she's not hooking up with anyone else and neither am I.

Deciding not to think too much into it tonight, I tuck the note into my bedside table drawer and close my eyes, letting sleep pull me under.

THE CAFÉ AT PALM SOUTH IS SMALL, but it's a chill place to eat. Usually, it's crawling with freshmen because their parents get sucked into buying the meal plan at orientation. By the time students get to their second year, they realize they'd rather get that two grand in an allowance from their parents so they can use three-hundred dollars of it to eat and the other seventeen-hundred to get shit-faced at Ralph's.

Filling my plate with an omelet, four pieces of toast, two pancakes, four slices of bacon and a tall glass of orange juice, I find the back corner booth and slide in. I used to sit here when I was a freshman and I chuckle thinking of the food fights I started from this spot, not to mention the girls I picked up.

"Thanks for slumming it," Cassie says as she slides into the booth across from me. Her bright hair is pulled into a low braid over her right shoulder and she plays with it absentmindedly as she organizes her tray. "My parents insisted on getting this stupid meal plan and now that I eat at the sorority house most of the time, I don't even use it."

"Hey, feel free to get me free food whenever you feel like it. I won't argue."

She blanches at the pile of food on my plate. "Yeah, I see that. Is someone else joining us or is that all for you?"

"Hey! A guy's gotta eat if he wants to make gains in the gym, Red."

Cassie freezes, her eyes snapping to mine. "Do *not* call me Red. Ever."

"Whoa. Did I hit a nerve?"

"It's just stupid. I have red hair, we all get it, no need to point it out with a nickname." She shoves a big bite of pancake into her mouth and licks the syrup off her bottom lip, wiping whatever smartass remark I planned on saying from my mind.

"I heard your roommate is being especially bitchy lately," I comment, changing the subject.

"How'd you hear about that?"

"Skyler told me."

She stills for a moment, her fork hovering over her plate, but almost quick enough for me not to notice before she takes another bite. "Oh.

Yeah. I don't know, I guess I shouldn't really care anymore."

"Of course you should care," I interject. "She was your best friend. No one's faulting you for caring about what happens to your friendship, Cassie."

Her pained eyes find mine. "I feel stupid for caring about her when she clearly couldn't care less about me."

"Hey." I reach across the table and grab her hand in mine. "It's her loss. She's a fucking moron if she doesn't see what a good friend you are. She'll regret burning this bridge when she's standing alone on that Zeta island, I can tell you that much."

Cassie chuckles, which makes me smile. That's the way I like to see her.

"You're silly."

"I'm also serious." I rub my thumb against hers and she glances up at me through her lashes. Realizing I'm probably holding on to the point of making it awkward, I pull back, cutting another bite off my pancake with my fork. "Just keep trying to make it work with her. If she doesn't try on her end by the time the semester is up, let her go and move into the KKB house. At that point, you know you did all you could to save the friendship and it was her decision to end it."

"Yeah, I think that's a good plan." She smiles. "Thanks, Adam."

"Anytime, Red." Cassie purses her lips and I bark out a loud laugh. "Kidding. So anyway, you going to semi-formal?"

"Of course I'm going. Why would I miss my own semi-formal?"

I shrug. "I don't know. I know some girls are weird about the whole going stag thing." Cassie shifts uncomfortably and I pause mid-bite. "Or do you have a date?"

"Uh, yeah. I'm going with someone."

"Who?" When she doesn't answer and her eyes skirt mine, I drop my fork completely and shove my plate forward. "Cassie. Please tell me you're not taking Clay."

"Why does it matter?"

"Because," I say exasperated, but can't figure out what to say next. "I told you. He's a dick."

"Well, he's really nice to me. And I assume you're going with Skyler, so why do you care?"

I scoff. "Yeah, I am going with Skyler. What does that have to do with anything?"

"Nothing." She sighs, gathering her leftover food items and piling them on her tray. "I have to go meet the girls. Thanks for breakfast."

I don't get the chance to say anything further before she's across the cafeteria and out the door.

Bear

"THIS IS BULLSHIT!" Josh yells and a few brothers join in with his assessment. I just cross my arms harder over my chest and kick back in my chair, shaking my head. This cannot be happening.

"No," Alec, the fuckhead alum who's ruining our lives interjects. "What's bullshit is that you asshats can't pull your own dick out of your ass long enough to realize worse will happen if you don't reign it in."

"We're in college," Josh argues. "Partying is part of that package."

"Maybe, but getting multiple sound violations, police calls, and write ups from the council aren't. If you want to still have letters to wear next year, you'll heed this warning and play ball our way for a while." The rest of the alumni brothers behind Alec all nod in unison, agreeing with this stupidity.

"Whatever. No parties for the rest of the semester. Got it. Are we through here?" I know I sound like an ungrateful dick, but on the inside I'm just as pissed off as my brothers. I get where the alumni brothers are coming from. Hell, I've been warning my Little all semester to get his shit together, but at the same time I'm not ready to give up parties completely. The fact that we're doing so without even being on suspension or probation is absolutely idiotic. The alumni want to teach us a lesson and also get our names off the radar. Whatever their reason, it sucks.

"If we're all at an understanding, then yes," Alec concedes. "Chapter is over."

"Great."

I stand before everyone else and jet out the door, shoving it a little harder than necessary when I exit. It bounces off the brick of our house before I slam it closed again and start off across campus toward the gym.

This is total, complete, utter bullshit. Horse shit. Fucking cow manure. I understand that we have to be careful and not do anything crazy enough to get our asses in the news, but throwing a few ragers and having too much fun shouldn't be a fucking crime. And Alec seems all too pleased to tell us we were on temporary probation. It's already November, so not throwing any parties for the next month doesn't seem like a big deal, but for us it's like asking us to cut our dicks off. Partying is what Omega Chi Beta does. It's who we are.

Fuck!

I punch a tall plastic sign advertising an event on campus and someone laughs. Spinning on my heels with a glare I know is murderous, I find Erin Xander sitting on one of the benches that line the main sidewalk leading to the gym.

"Whoa," she says, wide eyed. "Sorry. I've just never seen you so pissed." She puts her hands up in mock surrender. "Everything okay?"

Exhaling, I toss my gym bag to the ground and fall onto the bench next to her. "We just got put on temporary probation. No parties for the rest of the semester."

"Are you serious?" Erin runs her delicate hand through her dark blonde hair. "Wow. What are you guys going to do with yourselves? Isn't that like… all you do?"

"Exactly."

Erin Xander and I are nowhere near close. Really, I never talked to her much before I met Skyler. She's a cool chick, but she's way too spunky and involved for me. I've always been freaked out by women who like to juggle a thousand activities on top of school. Any girl who has to have control over that many things in life doesn't sound like a good time to me.

"Well, at least you can still *go* to parties. It's not total lockdown."

I scoff. "Who's going to throw parties like us?

Mu Beta Chi? Alpha Sigma?" That last option makes me roll my eyes. "Let's be real."

Erin giggles, but then stops abruptly and snaps her fingers. "Hey! I have a temporary fix. Come to semi-formal with me this weekend." I'm pretty sure I look at her as if she just sprouted a dick on her face because she instantly clarifies. "As *friends*, Bear. I've been too busy to even slightly worry about getting a date and I know all the other girls will have one. Come with me so I'm not stag. There will be plenty of booze and you know the Kappa Kappa Beta girls are a good time."

"Can't argue that," I concede, considering the option. The KKB semi-formal is always rumored to be a pretty decent party. I've never been before, and the thought of going with Erin kind of makes me want to shove my head into an ant pile, but then again Skyler will be there along with a bunch of my brothers. Kind of like moving the party, I guess. "Okay, I'm in."

Erin lifts her brows. "Yeah?"

"Why not? Free booze, sexy women all dressed up – sounds like a good time to me."

"Come to the house at six-thirty. We'll be taking a few buses over." She smiles, revealing her perfectly straight teeth that I'm sure her parents paid good money for. "And I'm wearing white."

I nod, snatching my bag off the ground and throwing it over my shoulder as I stand. "It's a date, Erin Xander." I wink and she shakes her head as I continue in the direction toward the gym.

Semi-formal isn't exactly what I have in mind when I think about partying, but it'll be fun, and anything is better than nothing. Pulling my phone from my pocket, I sigh when I see there's no missed calls or texts. Ever since I sent money home to both Carleton and my mom, I haven't heard a word. Not a peep. I must have ATM stamped on my forehead instead of SON and BROTHER.

As much as it irks me that I haven't heard from them, it's kind of a relief at the same time. Maybe that was it. Maybe they'll leave me alone now and I can focus on school and Omega Chi. Temporary probation is going to suck, but in a way, Alec is right – I can't imagine being on actual probation. Maybe we do need to take a step back and stay off the radar for a while. There's not much time left in the semester anyway. It can't be that bad, right?

Right?

Ashlei

I'M GOING TO BE SICK.

I'm literally going to vomit.

Holding the phone tight to my ear, the only thing keeping me from passing out is focusing hard on the breaths I'm taking. *In and out. Inhale and exhale.* Half of my brain is screaming that this can't be happening while the other half is scolding me for getting myself in this situation.

I fucked up.

Royally.

"Are you there?"

I swallow, but it feels like dry wood scraping my throat rather than saliva. "I'm here." I manage, raking my hands through my greasy hair. I need to shower. Ten minutes ago I was about to start getting ready for my semi-formal. Now, the thought of that seems so trivial.

"Do you understand what I'm saying to you?"

"Kya," I squeak her name, trying to reason. "You can't ask me for that kind of money. This isn't my fault and you know it. Hayden is the reason you lost that stash, not me. I had nothing to do with it."

"According to him, you did have something to do with it."

I groan, realizing that in a way, I did. "Listen, yeah, I fucked up and let him talk me into going up with him a few times but I swear I didn't know it was yours. I didn't know anything. I don't even know why I did it at all!" I scream. I'm panicking, I can't help it. "I told him to go fuck himself, Kya. I'm done with him and with that shit. You know me. You *know* this has never been my thing."

She sighs, and I can picture her pinching the bridge of her nose in frustration like she does when she's watching competition. "I love you, Ashlei. You're the best girl on our team right now – better than me, even. I'm not too proud to admit that. I wish I didn't have to do this, but now it's my ass on the line. You need to get me that money. I'm sorry."

"I don't have it, Kya!"

"Well, you've got rich ass parents and a sorority full of daddy's girls. I'm sure you can figure it out. I have to go."

"But what if I can't figure it out?"

The silence between us steals the breath from my chest as I wait for her to answer.

"You don't want the answer to that, Ashlei."

"Kya, wait. Seriously. We have to talk about this."

The line goes dead and I curse, throwing my cell across the yard. Tears sting the back of my eyes but I fight against them. In a way, I feel more numb than anything – like I'm living in a dream or someone else's life. This is *me*, Ashlei Daniels. I don't do drugs. I definitely don't do *stolen* drugs. I don't owe money to a drug dealer who owes her distributer. This isn't my life. It can't be.

"Gah," I hear a soft voice exclaim behind me. Bo plops down on the bench swing beside me and tucks her legs up, hugging them with her arms. "It's so cold!"

It's the first cold front of the season, if you can even call winter in Florida an actual season, and even with the sun still high in the sky it's just barely over fifty degrees. I was a little chilly when I answered the phone and stepped outside, but now my skin feels boiling hot.

I try to smile at Bo, but fail miserably and end up choking on a sob I should have seen coming. Bo's face immediately drops along with her legs and she quickly wraps me in a hug, her long dark hair falling all around me. "Oh my God, Lei. What happened?"

For a moment all I can do is cry, but I don't really even shed a tear. I'm sobbing, my face is twisted in pain, but no wetness pools in my eyes. I think I'm still in denial.

"I'm in trouble, Bo." I sniffle, pulling back from her grasp to align my eyes with hers. "Please, don't tell anyone. Not a soul. Not Jess, not anyone."

Bo shakes her head feverishly, her dark eyes wide. "I won't, I promise. What's going on?"

I chew my cheek, debating if I should even tell Bo. Up until now, these two sectors of my life have been kept completely separate. There's Palm South sorority girl Ashlei and there's pole dancing vixen Ashlei. Those two don't belong in the same world. They don't mix. They damn sure don't match.

"What would you say if I told you there's something about me that no one knows, not even my family?"

Bo smirks. "Honestly? I think we all know there's something you keep from us. It's just that no one pushes you on it."

I swallow. Am I really that obvious? I always felt like I did a decent job covering my tracks. "Okay, well, what if I told you that something that I've been hiding got me mixed up in something I always swore I would never do and now it's blown up in my face?"

"Lei," Bo stops me, reaching out to grab both of my hands in hers. Her long fingers are delicate, her hands soft and small, but she grips onto me firmly like she'll never let go. "Stop skirting around the issue and just tell me what happened. I'm not going to judge you. I love you." Her eyes grow wide at that and she quickly follows it with, "You're my sister."

"Okay," I say, expelling a long breath and letting my eyes fall to where our fingers are interlaced. "I'm just going to say this all really quickly and I'm not going to stop to look at you because if I do, I'll cry or scream or break down or something." I pause, waiting, and Bo just gives me a gentle squeeze. So I take one last breath and then put all my shit on the table.

"I started doing pole dance fitness over the summer and I'm really good at it and I've been sneaking off to practice and we won first in almost every category at a competition last month and now we're in the semi-finals in January and everything seems fine, right? Except that after I won I let this guy, Hayden, who I'm kind of sleeping with but not anymore talk me into doing cocaine which he does all the time and I swore I would never do but I did and I liked it and then I did it two more times with him but he pushed me out of a moving car because he was high and all of our friends thought it was hilarious because they were high, too, so I'm done with all of them but now Kya is saying that cocaine was actually her stash that she was supposed to be selling and Hayden stole it and now she owes her supplier money and I have to pay for half of the missing stash even though I only did it three times and I'm freaking out because I don't have that kind of money and I hate Hayden for making me do this but it's my own damn fault and fuck!" I can't say anything else after that last part, because in reality I know it is my fault that I'm in this situation. I screwed myself. I gave into peer pressure like a fucking thirteen-year-old.

I wait for Bo to gasp or pull back or shake her head, especially after I just expelled all that shit in one long exhausted breath. I wait for *any* kind of reaction. After a moment, she only squeezes my hands tighter and ducks her head a little low, urging me to look at her. When I do lift my eyes to hers, all I see is compassion and understanding.

"How much do you owe her?"

"A lot." I sigh. "Ten-thousand, to be exact."

Bo whistles under her breath. "I'm assuming parents are out of the question?" I nod. She pulls her hands from mine and runs them through her hair, thinking. "Well, I have to say I was not expecting to hear any of that from you." I cross my arms over my chest defensively, wishing I could crawl into a hole. "But you know what? You'll figure this out. We can do a fundraiser or sell some of your designer clothes and bags. You probably have ten grand in shoes alone."

I chuckle at that. "That's pretty accurate, I think."

"See!" Bo smiles, placing her hand gently on my knee. I shiver, but something tells me it's not from the cool breeze. "I know it feels like a lot right now, and to be honest – it is. It's not something you can ignore or take lightly. But at the same time, there's nothing you can do about it right at this moment. You'll need some time to get your thoughts figured out and your plan together."

"I just don't even know where to start."

"Start by going to formal with me," she whispers. She gazes up at me through her dark lashes and blushes slightly. My stomach knots instantly. "I'm going stag and I know you are, too, so let's just go together. Take the night off and don't think about all this shit. What's this Kya girl going to do anyway?"

"She told me I didn't want the answer to that question."

Bo scoffs. "I'm sure she's just trying to save her own ass, Lei." Another cool gust of wind brushes both of our hair back and off our shoulders and Bo curses. "Damn, it's getting colder." Her soft dark eyes find mine and she rubs her arms through her long sleeve shirt. "Come inside with me. Let's put on pretty dresses and dance the night away. Then tomorrow, I'll help you figure out where to start. Sound like a plan?"

Just a few minutes ago, it felt like my entire world was crashing down around me. How did Bo make something that felt so heavy suddenly feel like nothing at all?

"I don't know how much fun I'll be," I admit, but I stand nonetheless.

Bo smiles mischievously. "Just break out your stripper moves. I bet that'll get the party started." She smacks my ass playfully and skips inside while my mouth hangs open. Quickly, I retrieve my phone from where it landed in the yard and trot off after her.

The last thing I want to do is get dressed up and pretend like I'm not in deep shit, but the way Bo was looking at me has my curiosity running wild. I could dwell on my misfortune or I could dive deeper into what unsaid words lay behind her soft chocolate irises.

Yeah.

Option two sounds a *lot* more fun.

Adam

THE KAPPA KAPPA BETA girls are fucking crazy.

After pre-gaming for an hour, we all piled into the charter buses and continued partying the entire drive to the hotel where the dance is being held. It's not even eight yet but one of the Omega Chi brothers already threw up in his date's purse trying to keep up with the shenanigans. I, on the other hand, am just trying to figure out how to hide my boner as we make our way inside the large venue. Skyler was rubbing up against me and kissing my neck the entire ride here.

To say I'm a little worked up would be an understatement.

"God, it's freezing," Cassie says, crossing her arms tightly and shivering. "Leave it to Florida to give us our first cold night when we're all in dresses."

Skyler laughs. "I don't know, I'm actually kind of warm after that bus ride." She winks at me with that last line and I shake my head. The girl has no shame.

And it's so hot.

Skyler's soft brown hair cascades down past her shoulders, curling just a bit at the ends. Her makeup is dark and intense, making her icy blue eyes stand out even more than usual. She's wearing a skin tight crimson dress that matches the lipstick she was smearing all over my skin on the bus and her heels make her almost as tall as me. I don't give a shit, though, because her legs look fucking incredible.

Cassie, on the other hand, has her hair tied up into a soft up-do with tiny tendrils framing her face. She's dressed in a floor-length white dress that accents her slender frame along with the innocence she seems to wear like an accessory everywhere she goes. Where Skyler's makeup is fierce and sexy, Cassie's is minimal and simplistic.

One is in red, one is in white.

The devil and the angel.

When Clay doesn't offer Cassie his coat, I roll my eyes and fight back the words I'd like to say to him, shrugging off my own jacket instead. "Here," I say, hanging it over her shoulders. "Better?"

Cassie pulls the front of my coat tight around her and visibly sighs at the warmth. "Much." She turns to me, a curious look in her green eyes. "Thank you."

It doesn't take long for us to reach the front of the hotel and as soon as we're inside the large glass doors, we're immediately shielded from the brisk air. The hotel is lavish with gold and navy accents, giving the atmosphere a regal feel. We're ushered into the main ballroom and one of the waiters shows us where the bathrooms are as well as the bars. I follow Skyler and some of her sisters to claim a table before we head for the closest one.

No time to waste.

"I kind of want to skip all of this and fast forward to the part where we're in your bed. Is that bad of me?" Skyler asks, her voice just above a whisper as she kisses right behind my ear. I grip her small waist firmly in my hands and meet her lips with mine.

"Kind of. But I like you better when you're bad."

She smiles against my lips before kissing me swiftly and turning just as the bartender asks her order. "Vodka tonic, please."

"Captain and Coke for me," I chime in, propping my elbows up and leaning back on the edge of the bar. Scanning the room and taking in the scenery, I spot Clay and Cassie at our table. He peels my jacket off her shoulders and tosses it over a chair haphazardly, smirking when her cleavage is more visible. She's barely showing any skin at all, but it's enough to drive a guy crazy, that's for sure. I can tell she's still shivering slightly, but she doesn't reach for my coat again. She just links her arm through his and follows him to the back of the line at the small bar across from where ours is.

I shake my head. I shouldn't be watching Cassie so closely, but I fucking hate Clay and I know there's only one thing he could want from her. The thought that he might actually get it literally makes me sick. She's too good for him. How does she not see that?

"Let's dance," Skyler yells over the music the DJ just started, throwing back a shot before handing another to me. I follow her lead, swallowing what I'm pretty sure is vodka and letting it burn the entire way down before following her back to our table. We take a couple of pulls from our mixed drinks before leaving them on the table and moving to the dance floor.

Skyler places her hand in mine and I twirl her out and back into me before wrapping my arms around her waist. Slowly, she winds her body, turning to face away from me and pressing her ass into me. My hands roam her body before gripping her hips and I move in time with the music and the tempo she's setting.

Damn. Now I kind of want to skip this shit, too.

After a few songs, we're already working up a sweat and I'm ready to finish my rum. Just as we leave the dance floor and make our way back to the table, Clay leads Cassie past us and out onto the space we just left open. My eyes find hers just as Clay grips her ass hard, pulling her close and grinding against her. I clench my jaw and quickly look away, reaching for my drink and draining the rest of it in one pull.

"Round two?" Skyler asks, eying my now empty glass. She chugs the rest of her drink and I do my damndest to keep my eyes on her and off the situation on the dance floor.

"Let's do another shot."

Skyler thrusts her hands into the air. "That's what I'm talking about!" Laughing, she grabs my hand and leads me through the crowd and back to the bar. I don't let myself look at Clay and Cassie again. I'm here with Skyler. Cassie and I are just friends. She can do whatever the hell she wants with whoever the hell she wants. It's none of my business.

But then why does it feel like it is?

Jess

"THIS BLOWS," I say, sucking down the last of my rum punch. I signal to the bartender for another and Erin laughs.

"It's not that bad, Jess. At least you have Matt here."

I cringe and immediately drink half of my new drink. "Don't remind me. He's been pawing at my chest like a middle schooler all damn night."

"Hey, you're getting action tonight. Be thankful. Some of us came with friends," she reminds me, nodding her head toward where Clinton is chatting with a few of his brothers. He looks absolutely delicious in the simple black and white tuxedo he's donning and I shake my head.

"How you're sticking to that friends-only rule with him looking like that is beyond me."

"Jess!" Erin squeals, her blonde curls bouncing. "It's _Bear_, for God's sake."

"And? Bear's hot!"

"He's practically like Skyler's brother."

"Again, and? That doesn't mean he's your brother."

Erin seems to chew on that along with her straw as she sips on her drink, still staring across the room at Clinton and his brothers. Suddenly, Matt slides up and wraps his arms around my waist. Even though he's a decent lay, I still inwardly groan and roll my eyes.

Because all I can think about is how he's *not* Jarrett.

Bastard.

"Let's dance."

"I'd rather not," I say bluntly.

Erin chuckles and I subtly flick her the bird.

"Wanna sneak off and find a closet somewhere then?" Matt smirks and bites his lip but the second the word *closet* leaves his lips my ovaries react. I'd like to find one, alright, but only if Jarrett is inside it.

Fuck!

"Sorry, I need to go…" I consider telling him I need to fix my hair or powder my nose but decide against it. "Piss."

At that, he grimaces and I offer a sweet smile, pulling away from his grasp and making my way across the room. I drain the rest of my drink and leave the empty glass on a table as I pass.

When I reach the bathroom, I splash my face with cold water and lean against the counter, shaking my head. *This is impossible.* As much as I try to deny it, Jarrett has invaded my every thought. He's right – none of these little boys can fuck me the way he does. God, just thinking about it makes me squirm. If there weren't several other stalls occupied in here I'd probably just rub one out and be done with it.

The uncomfortable ache that I usually have no issue handling is building even more as I exit the bathroom. I notice Skyler and Bear talking outside the tall glass doors in front of the hotel and I smile. It's about time they worked out whatever the hell has been going on between them. I can't decide if they act like an old married couple or siblings or both.

I'm just rounding the corner to the hallway that leads back to the main room when I hear a breathy giggle. Halting, I back up a few steps to peer down the opposite hall that leads away from the bathrooms. I smile, happy at least someone is getting their kicks tonight.

Slowly, and as quietly as I can, I tiptoe a little further down the hall and peek around the corner where I heard the noise. I'm still hidden behind the wall, but I just barely make out the hem of Ashlei's long, glittery coral dress. *Damn, Lei! Get it!* I fight back laughter as I spy more, leaning my head out further so I can get a glimpse of whoever's date she stole. I know she came here stag, so who's the mystery man?

I bite my lips between my teeth and cringe as the beads of my dress just barely scrape against the wall, making a soft scratching noise. Ashlei and her man friend don't even blanch, though, so I lean out even further.

And then I gasp.

Slamming my hand hard over my mouth, I tuck myself back around the corner and press my back against the wall.

"What was that?" Ashlei asks and I slowly skirt the wall down the hall, desperately trying to keep my cool. When I reach the end of the hall I give up trying to be quiet and quickly cut across the lobby, flying out the door where Bear and Skyler are still talking.

"J-Love?" Skyler asks but I don't turn. "Where are you going?"

I don't answer, I just jump in one of the waiting cabs in the car-pool area and tell him to drive. I spout off the name of the beach bar before I even realize what I'm doing, but I don't take it back. My breath is labored, my heart beating rapidly out of my chest. No way did I just see that. No fucking way did I just see Ashlei making out with... with...

Oh, God, what's the point?!

PALM SOUTH UNIVERSITY 1

I know exactly what I saw. Ashlei was getting action, alright. She had her tongue down someone's throat and she had her hands on their body.

But it wasn't any guy I know.

It wasn't any guy at all.

It was my Little.

Bear

I'M GLAD I LET ERIN coax me into going to semi-formal with her. More than half of my brothers are here and my theory about the girls looking hot as fuck turned out to be extremely accurate. I'm not a fan of putting on a tuxedo by any means, but for a non-Omega Chi party, this shit's not bad.

Matt excuses himself from our group, murmuring something about bagging Jess as he cuts toward the bar just as my phone pings. Frowning at the all-caps text from my mom, I quickly call her.

"I'm outside."

"What?" I yell against the noise, plugging the ear opposite my phone.

"I'm outside, Clinton."

Scanning the room, I find the opening that leads out into the lobby and across to the large glass doors at the front of the hotel. Sure as shit, my mom is standing just beyond them. Her slight frame looks even smaller under the grand doors with gold trim, her over-sized t-shirt hanging nearly down to her knees.

Ending the call, I shove my phone back in my pocket and briskly cross the room. I'm trying to calm down, but I'm pissed. Why the fuck is my mom showing up to the KKB semi-formal? Why is she in Florida, period?

The chilly air immediately hits me as I push through the outer doors, cooling my hot skin. "What are you doing here?"

"That's the first thing you have to say to me?" she asks, her face falling a little. She looks strung out, her skin ashen and her hair a mess. I have no doubt she's been using and the first thing I think of is my little brother.

"Where's Clayton?"

She sighs, shaking her head. "Your brother is fine. Well, your younger one, anyway. He's staying with some friends in Pittsburgh."

"Which brings me back to my first question."

My mom waits for sympathy to show on my face, but it's nowhere in sight. I can't feel sorry for her anymore. That passed after I turned sixteen.

"Clinton, I need some money. Carleton is in the car." She turns, pointing back to an idling, beat up piece of shit Cadillac. "We're in some trouble and we need a way out. Now I know what you're thinking," she says before I have the chance to cut her off. "And I'm telling you, we're getting clean after this. Carleton wants his baby boys to have a father they can look up to and I'm tired of this shit ruining my life. But we aren't going to have the chance to get clean if you don't help us, you understand?" Her eyes hit me hard with that last line and I understand all too well.

"What the fuck, Mom?!" I run my hands over my head, frustrated. "What the hell did you do?!"

"I'm not getting into that with you. You don't care, anyway."

"Oh? And what, you don't owe me an explanation for having to ask for money from me... *again*? Or how about for the fact that you haven't talked to me one fucking time since I sent you money last time?"

"We've never been close, Clinton. Stop acting like I'm the big bad mom in this situation."

"The big? The?" I laugh, my hysterics reaching an all-time high as I try to repeat what she just said but fail. "Do you hear yourself?"

"Please, Clinton," she begs just as the doors open behind me.

"Bear?" It's Skyler, and now I'm even more pissed. My life at Palm South is not my life back home. In fact, the person I was before college doesn't exist anymore. I don't want anyone – especially not Skyler – seeing where I came from. Or *who* I came from.

"You need to go," I say firmly, my jaw hard.

Mom nods, at least having enough common sense to not push the subject now that Skyler is present. "Just please, help your family, Clinton. Consider what will happen if you don't." She swallows and I shake my head in warning. "We're staying at the Motel 8 down the road."

With that, she turns and jumps back in the car and I'm left with Skyler. I know she wants to ask what happened, but she doesn't – she just walks up and leans her head on my arm. After a moment, she asks, "That your mom?"

I nod.

"You don't look anything like her."

I don't know why, but for some reason, hearing her say those words makes me smile. Skyler shivers a bit against me and I pull her into me, wrapping my arms around her shoulder and burying my nose in her hair. She smells like nothing I've ever smelled before, something too clean and put together for my life.

"You can talk to me, Bear. I know it may seem like I won't understand, but I might surprise you."

Sighing, I don't even try to fight it anymore. I spill everything. I trust Skyler more than anyone else at this school and she's done nothing but prove time and time again that she's a great friend. So, I tell her about my shitty past – about my mom, my brother, the drugs, the money, my little brother caught in the middle of it – everything. When I finish, she pulls back, crossing her arms over her chest.

"They need money again?"

"Yeah. Who knows how much this time."

Skyler chews her bottom lip so hard I think she might draw blood and then quickly reaches for her clutch. Pulling out a slender wallet and a pen, Skyler scribbles out something and tears the small sheet of paper away, handing it out for me to take. "Here."

When I pull it under the light shining from inside the hotel, I realize it's a check.

For two-thousand dollars.

"What the fuck, Skyler?" I shake my head, thrusting it back to her. "No. Hell no."

"Bear, hear me out."

"No! First of all, who even has checks anymore?"

Skyler laughs. "I send money home to my family all the time. Checks are the easiest and safest way to do that."

At that, my hand drops to my side, the check still firmly grasped between my fingers. "What? How often?"

"At least once a month." She shrugs. "They don't ask me for it, but I send it anyway."

I don't have words for that little nugget of information. I knew Skyler had a strange family situation at home, I knew she entered poker tournaments all the time for a reason, but I had no idea she was sending money home that frequently.

"Give that to your mom, Bear. Tell her that's it, that's all she's ever getting from you again, and call it done. They'll get themselves out of whatever trouble they're in and you can breathe easy knowing you don't have to drain your savings."

"This is too much," I say, shaking my head and staring down at her neat handwriting.

"Psh," she says, waving her hands. "I can make that back in a weekend at the downtown casino. No sweat." She winks and I know she's lying, but she's trying her best to make me feel okay with this situation.

"Why Skyler?"

"Why am I helping you?" I nod. "Are you kidding, Bear? Your family may be fucked up, but what you don't realize is that you're *my* family now, too. And families help each other – always. That's why you have always helped your mom and your brother, and that's why I'm helping you now."

"I don't know what to say."

"Don't say anything. Call your mom, have her come back to pick up this check, and then get back in there and drink with me."

Still staring at her like everything she's saying to me is completely ludicrous, I pull her in for a crushing hug. She laughs against my chest and wraps her small arms around me, too. "I love you, Bear."

"I love you, Sky."

"Hey," she says, pulling back. "What are you doing for Thanksgiving?"

I shrug. "Probably staying on campus with some of my brothers."

"Will you come home with me? Meet my parents and my older brother? Please?"

"What is this, Bear Charity Case Night?"

She chuckles. "No, I just want them to meet my new brother." At that, I return her smile and kiss her forehead.

"You have a knack for making a big guy feel really small, you know that?"

Skyler opens her mouth to respond just as the doors beside us fly open and Jess tears across the parking lot. Skyler calls out after her but Jess doesn't stop. She hops into one of the waiting cabs and before we have the chance to digest it, she's gone.

"Well shit," Skyler says. "Wonder what that's about."

I sigh. "Omega Chi parties never have this much drama."

Skyler barks out a laugh and punches my arm. "Yeah, yeah, whatever. Call your mom and come back inside."

After Skyler leaves, I do call my mom back. I make Carleton get out of the car with her and I stare both of them in the eyes when I hand them the check and threaten that this is the last time they better ever contact me for money. They both seem insanely grateful, but I know it's just temporary. As much as I want to believe they won't ask me for money again, I know they will.

But tonight, I don't let that thought hold me down. After their car leaves, I make my way back inside and Erin slides me a new drink as soon as I reach our table.

"I've been looking for you."

I cock a brow. "Yeah?"

She smiles, her light brown eyes shimmering in the soft light of the ballroom. Her dark blonde hair that's usually hanging to her shoulders is pinned up in an organized mess of curls and it accents her slender face. She always looks classic and traditional, but tonight she looks royal. "Yeah. I want to dance."

"Well, it is your ball, princess." I wink and chug down the rest of my Hennessey before letting her drag me to the floor. And then I dance and drink and laugh until I forget everything else.

Everything except Skyler.

I'll never forget that girl.

Adam

SKYLER HAS BEEN OUTSIDE with Bear for almost half an hour now, and that means I'm finding it harder and harder to ignore Clay's douchebag ways. Pair that with the fact that I'm two shots past drunk and you could say I'm not exactly in the best state of mind right now.

Clay spots me watching him and Cassie dancing and he whispers something in her ear, making her giggle and me growl before excusing himself. Moments later, he slides up next to me at the bar, but I don't even turn to acknowledge him. Even without looking directly at him, I can see his douchey Ken doll smirk.

"Having fun, Brooks?"

"Yep." I let the end of the word pop as I take a large drink from my glass. "You?"

"Oh yeah. But I guess you already know that since you've been watching me all night, huh?"

I shake my head, finally turning to face him. The cocky grin plastered on his face makes me snarl my next sentence. "I don't fucking like you being around Cassie."

"Oh, I'm sorry – did I ask for your permission?"

"She's a good girl, Clay. I'm serious. Don't fuck her around."

"Didn't plan on it," he says, sipping from the shot glass the bartender just slid him. He props his elbows up on the bar and scans the room until he finds Cassie. "Now fuck her up and down every inch of my room tonight? Definitely."

"Goddamnit, Clay!" I growl, slamming my glass down hard on the bar. He just cackles and I grit my teeth before storming across the room. Cassie's eyes widen as I approach her but I don't say a word, I just hook her by the inside of her elbow and drag her out to the hallway near the bathrooms.

"What the hell, Adam?"

"You can't leave with Clay tonight."

Her mouth pops open. "Oh my God, are you serious right now?" Her green eyes take on a more hazel look under the low light of the hotel and she crosses her arms, popping one hip to the side. It's the sassiest I've ever seen her.

"Yes, I'm dead serious. He just wants to get in your pants, Cassie."

"Well, I guess it's lucky for him that I'm not wearing any pants tonight, huh?" She rolls her eyes and tries to stride past me but I pull her back.

"Damnit, this isn't a game!"

"And you're not my boyfriend!"

I blanch. "That's not what this is about."

"Oh?" she asks, stepping closer. "It's not?"

Swallowing, I search her eyes for the hundreds of questions that lay hidden behind that one she posed. The air between us feels thicker, charged with an energy I can't quite determine. "I'm just looking out for you. Can't you just trust me when I say he's bad news?"

"He's been nothing but nice to me," she murmurs softly, still not stepping out of my space. Reaching out, I let my hands just barely rest on her arms.

"He knows what he's doing, Cassie. He's good at it."

Her brows pull together, and for a moment I think she might listen to me, but then she shakes her head and pulls back just as Clay emerges from the ballroom. "I can handle myself, Adam."

"Everything okay?" Clay asks, faking a concern I know he doesn't have.

"Yeah. You ready to get out of here?" Cassie asks.

"Absolutely." Clay tosses his jacket over his shoulder and throws his other arm around hers. Cassie glances at me once more before turning toward the door, and then it's Clay who looks at me. With a smirk, he winks, pulls Cassie closer, whispers in her ear and bites her earlobe. She leans into him, giggling, and I curse, punching the padded wall outside the main room just as he tosses back his head with a laugh and walks her through the large glass doors.

I'm still frustrated when I snap for the bartender's attention back at the bar. Skyler reappears, looking just as gorgeous as ever, and wraps her arms around my neck. Desperate, I pull her in for a long, hard kiss, tangling my hands in her hair as she moans against my mouth.

Cassie is my friend and I do care about her, but I can't make her decisions for her. I can't make her *mistakes* for her either. I may have lost my cool, but there's nothing I can do to take any of it back now. Instead, I'm just going to focus on the beautiful girl wrapped around me and the sounds she'll be making in my bed later tonight.

Cassie McBee is on her own.

Jess

IT'S A LONGER CAB RIDE from the hotel to the beach than from campus, but it gives me time to think. No matter how hard I try, I can't get the image of what I saw earlier out of my head. Maybe I should have called them both out on it right then and there, but I didn't have the balls. I mean, how often do you see your best friend and your Little making out in the back of semi-formal?

It's not even the kissing that bothers me. At least, I don't think so. I mean, I'm not exactly cool with it, but then again, whatever – who am I to judge, right? But why did they have to lie to me? Bo's been making me feel like shit about how we never hang out and Ashlei has been sneaking around at all hours of the night. Is that where she's been going? To be with Bo?

God, just thinking about it makes my blood boil.

What's with all the fucking secrets around here?!

I let everyone in on my dirty laundry. Hell, not only do I hang it up to dry in front of all my sisters but I practically ask them to take pictures and post them on social media. I couldn't give two shits what they think about my scandals. Maybe that's where I'm doing it wrong. I missed the memo about not sharing shit with your fucking sisters.

When the cab finally pulls up to the bar, I toss two twenties over the seat and bolt for the door. Jarrett sees me before I even make it to the entrance. I'm not sure if it's because he knows me or just because he knows my body but as soon as his eyes meet mine, he drops the glass he's cleaning. Planting one hand hard on the bar, he balances himself and jumps up and over the bar. He strides toward me purposefully and tosses the small white bar towel behind him just in time to catch me as I jump into his arms and wrap my legs around him, crashing my mouth down on his.

"Are you finally done with those little boys?" His voice is low, husky, needy.

I kiss him harder, fisting his shirt in my hands and not giving two fucks if anyone is watching us. "I'm done with everyone."

Jarrett doesn't ask questions. He doesn't poke and prod to get me to talk to him. He doesn't tell anyone inside the bar that he's leaving or that he'll be right back. He just carries me back out the door, across the parking lot, and out to the beach. Dropping me down onto one of the cushioned beach chairs owned by the bar, he rips his board shorts down to his ankles and pushes my short, mint green dress up to my hips. He wastes no time, tearing a condom wrapper open with his teeth and rolling it down over his massive cock before burying himself inside me.

And then, everything else is lost. Jarrett's hands and mouth completely own me. They take me down, pull me under, push me deep into the earth until there's nothing and no one left but me and him.

Just the way I like it.

Episode 6

"I DON'T WANT THIS TO BE COMPLICATED"

Erin

I CAN'T REMEMBER the last time I had a hangover, but my eyes aren't even open yet and my head is hammering away in my skull. It's safe to say I have one now. Groaning, I squeeze my eyes shut tighter and pull the fluffy, light blue covers up and over my head. When they're jerked back, I bolt upright.

What the hell?

Slowly craning my neck to the side, I squeak and scurry from the bed, taking the covers with me and quickly wrapping them around my chest.

"Fuck, Josh, stop messing around!" Clinton sprawls out, naked as the day he was born, stretching his legs and wiggling his toes. I swallow as the tight muscles of his abdomen ebb and flow with the movement. His dark skin is a vast contrast against my cream sheets and my eyes can't help but fall to the cut V that leads right down to another part of his body coming to attention this morning. When his eyes open and he finds me cowering in the corner and staring at him wide-eyed, he blanches. "Erin?"

"Bear."

We just stare at each other for a moment in disbelief. Slowly, our eyes scan my room, surveying his clothes in a pile on the floor and my dress thrown over the back of my desk chair. Ashlei's bed is still made from the day before, which means she probably didn't come home at all.

Which also means I was alone with Bear all night.

As if I just emerged from beneath a salty wave, my eyes clear and I remember in blurry, yet surprisingly vivid details what happened after semi-formal last night.

I snuck Clinton inside. We made out. He ripped my dress off. There was some sort of talk about stopping that neither of us listened to. And we had sex.

We totally, *totally* had sex.

"Did we?"

I nod. "Uh, yep."

Clinton's brows furrow and he pinches the bridge of his nose. "Well, shit."

All at once, I spring into action, gathering his clothes off the floor and shoving them toward him before pulling on a pair of shorts and sleep shirt to cover my still-naked body. "You have to get out of here. Mom Cindy is going freak out if she finds you here." I shake my head, cracking my door open just enough to peek down the hall before turning back to Clinton. "Oh my God. I can't believe this happened."

"Relax," he says groggily, pulling on his last dress shoe. He left the belt off his slacks and his white dress shirt is unbuttoned at the top. With his tie and jacket in one hand, he moves toward the door where I'm still standing. "It's fine. We had a few drinks and then had a little fun. No harm, no foul, right?"

My heart is beating rapidly against my rib cage and I can't seem to find enough breath even though I know I'm inhaling and exhaling over and over again. Skyler would probably kill me if she found out this happened. And the other girls would totally judge. It's *Clinton* we're talking about here. Plus, I'm trying to move up in the sorority – I can't do that if word gets out that I'm sneaking boys into the house.

"Bear… we can't…"

"I know. I won't say anything."

"Like, *no one* can find out."

"Erin, it's fine," he assures me again. Holding up two fingers, he cocks a brow. "No one hears a peep about it. Scout's honor. Okay?"

I nod. "Okay. I won't tell anyone either."

At that, Clinton smirks. "Obviously."

Placing his free hand on the door handle, Clinton glances back at the bed and it's as if he remembers what happened, too, because he smiles a little broader and throws me a wink before disappearing down the hall. Forcing the door shut behind him, I press my back against it and let out a mixture of a moan and a sigh, shaking my head.

That did *not* just happen.

I can feel myself hyperventilating. I don't have control of this situation. I *clearly* didn't have control of anything last night. I need something I can exercise power over and fast. Right now I'm spinning, losing balance, and this is not me. This is not Erin Xander.

The last time I let myself lose control of my emotions and actions was the summer before my senior year of high school. It was the summer I visited my grandparents in Kansas and in a way, I found myself in those short two months – but I also lost myself, too. I shiver, the blue eyes of a boy I haven't thought about in a long time sneaking up on me out of nowhere. I vowed after that shit show that I would always have a plan and more than that – I would always stick to said plan.

Hooking up with Clinton was *not* in my plan.

Quickly, I cross the room and rip my laptop from its power cord before falling back onto my bed. Before I can process it, I'm feverishly typing out my essay for my Recruitment Chair application. I was hesitant about applying, since usually executive positions are reserved for seniors, but I'm too impatient to wait around for the presidency and I don't want a small chair position. I want to lead. I want authority.

More than that, I need it.

As if my morning couldn't get any worse, my phone rings and my mom's picturesque face fills the screen. Though her hair is dark unlike my own, I definitely inherited my high cheek bones and chocolate eyes from her. I pray every day that I don't inherit anything else – especially characteristically.

She's ensuring my arrival for Thanksgiving, no doubt, especially since they're hosting their annual dinner at the country club. Just the thought of making small talk with my parents' friends and listening to Mom and Dad's incessant pleas for me to find a suitable man make me want to crawl under my bed and die. *If only they knew about last night…*

I laugh out loud at that and silence my phone at the same time. I can call her back later, and she will definitely *never* know about last night. I can't even imagine the lecture I'd get if she ever did find out.

What *is* Bear's major? Football? Beer? Mind-blowing Sex?

Shit. Did I really just think that?

Typing faster, I set my focus back to the task at hand – on something I have control over. I can't help what my parents feel about me or take back my actions from last night, but I can take over what will happen when I get back from Thanksgiving.

I'll be elected Recruitment Chair, ace my finals, party with my sisters and then take off for a European Christmas trip with Kelsey. I had a little too much fun last night, but now it's back to business.

And, this time, no straying from the plan.

Skyler

THANKSGIVING IS BY FAR my favorite holiday. For most families, it means turkey dinner, football, and Black Friday shopping. For mine, it means homemade pizza, craft beer, and poker.

Absolute perfection.

Having Clinton with me this year makes it even more special. I was slightly terrified on our drive up, realizing he was going to be walking into a completely different atmosphere than the one at Palm South, but then I realized it's Clinton – he's the last one I have to worry about judging me. If anything, it seems like Clinton came from a similar situation – if not a worse one.

I may have never had money or nice things growing up, but I always knew my family loved me.

I'm not sure Clinton can say the same.

That thought wrecks me as I watch him working in the kitchen with my mom. I can tell it's his first time making a homemade pizza because he's having trouble with the dough just like I did the first time I made it. I can't help but chuckle at his determined scowl as his large fingers work against the sticky concoction, not really making any progress at all until Mom jumps in to help. He just grunts and takes a long swig of his IPA.

My parents' house is small but homey, and I think I love it even more for that. There are family photos on every wall and not one shelf or coffee table is clear of clutter. Mail, magazines, and other odds and ends cover the dining room table and car keys and wallets sit alongside vases and knick-knacks on the mantel. The forest green and cream white colored accents in the living room don't really match any of the furniture and the kitchen is an explosion of tonight's dinner ingredients and dishes. The fridge is hidden by mismatched magnets and takeout menus and not one plate matches another in the cabinet. I love my home, and I love Clinton being in it even more.

"He seems like a great guy," Dad says, placing his rough hands on my shoulders and squeezing. He's a tall, lean man with light blonde hair slowly graying at the ends. The wrinkles on his face tell the world that he's had to work hard in his life but the smile he always has plastered on says he's enjoyed every last minute. He gave me my favorite feature – my ocean blue eyes. "I can tell he cares about you."

"It's not like that, Dad," I clarify, patting his

hand with my own. "We're just friends. But he is really special to me."

"I see that." Dad plants a kiss on the top of my head and adjusts his glasses just as Clinton removes his hands where he's just kneaded out the dough. He curses as it folds back in on itself and Dad chuckles. "Let's go help them or we're never going to eat."

After dinner, Mom and my older brother, Skott, start setting the table up for our poker game. Skott is seven years older than me and lives in Alaska. He works for a wildlife preservation society and the fact that he even got the time to come home for the holiday is amazing. With his long, disheveled brown hair and newly sprouted beard, he looks nothing like what I remember. Then again, I haven't seen him other than the occasional video chat in almost two years. His blue eyes are still the same, though – they match mine and Dad's. When he ruffles my hair as I pull the last dirty dish from the table, I smile and stick out my tongue at him before brushing past.

"Your family is amazing," Clinton says as he dries another dish. I start scrubbing the one I just retrieved and smile.

"Yeah, they are. Definitely far from the other families of Palm South though, huh?"

Clinton shares my smile, shaking his head. "That's an understatement. I can definitely say I'd rather be here playing poker with your family than playing golf with one of my brothers'."

"Or drinking tea."

"Or browsing the newest BMW line."

I hand him the last dish to dry and whip out my best attempt at a rich southern accent, which kind of sounds more like a hick because I have no idea what I'm doing. "Or sitting around talking about how perfect our houses are."

Clinton laughs, but mimics me, his accent more European. "Or comparing trust funds like dicks."

My mom walks in just as he finished the sentence and she blushes, her dark chocolate hair falling in her face a bit as she hands us a dish I must have missed. "It's okay, Bear. No need to prove to us how big your... *trust fund* is."

Dad and Skott crack up at that and I can't help but join them. Even though his dark skin doesn't show it, I swear Clinton is blushing as he apologizes to my mom. She pats him on the arm and then we all gather around the table as Dad divvies out the chips and explains the blinds. Clinton watches poker and plays at the casino with me sometimes, so luckily we don't have to teach him how to play the game itself.

"Ready for me to take all your money, sis?" Skott asks as Dad deals the first hand.

"Keep dreaming," I tease.

The rest of the night is a mixture of laughter and good conversation, both of which I appreciate. It's been so long since I've been able to let loose without thinking about what guys are around or what my sisters might be thinking. I can tell Clinton is enjoying himself, too, and I know he needs the break from life just as much as I do. Neither of us have even really been on our phones, other than me responding to Adam's texts and Clinton following up with his mom – who still hasn't reached out to him since semi-formal.

I take everyone's money by the end of the evening. Dad and Mom aren't surprised in the slightest but Skott fought me until the end. He's still a little bitter when he knuckles my head and slinks down the hall to his old bedroom. Clinton and I opt to sit on my front porch for a while, talking a bit but mostly just enjoying the nice November weather and listening to the soft buzz of insects.

When we go back to campus, it'll be finals and elections and then we'll all disperse for Christmas break. It's kind of nice to just take a moment to enjoy life without all the rush that goes along with being in college.

Too bad it's short lived.

I'M QUIET ON THE RIDE HOME Sunday, though my thoughts are loud in my head. After the first hour passes, Clinton finally breaks the silence.

"Are you going to tell me what you're thinking so hard about?" When I don't answer immediately, he sighs. "Skyler, what's going on? Did Adam say something? Everything was fine, we were having a great weekend. What changed?"

"Shit," I groan, sliding my hands down to the bottom of the steering wheel and stretching my back out against the scratchy seat. Since everything is so close to campus at Palm South, I always leave my car at home and take cabs or buses around the university, so I rented a car for the drive home and back. The small economic car isn't nearly as comfortable as my old beat up Pontiac, though. "My parents are in trouble, Bear."

"What do you mean? They seemed fine to me."

"I found a letter from the bank in the stack of mail my mom gave me. She must have gotten theirs mixed in with mine. It was a warning letter." I sigh. "They're about to lose the house."

Clinton blanches. "Holy shit."

"Yeah."

He looks out the window for a short moment before shaking his head. "Damn it, Skyler. You shouldn't have given me that money. Your family needs it just as much as mine does. And at least yours isn't using it for fucking pills."

"Don't, Bear," I warn. "I gave you that because I care about you and I wanted that situation to be squashed. I wouldn't take it back now even if you tried, and you know it." Sighing, I brace myself for what I'm about to say next. "I just need to figure out a new plan."

Clinton cocks a brow, curious. "You say that like you already have one."

"I do. Well, kind of."

"What do you mean?"

I sigh again. "There's a huge tournament over Christmas break in Atlantic City. It's not like what I usually play, Bear." I pause, shaking my head at the audacity I have for even thinking I have a chance at this. "The pros will be there. There's a lot of money at stake and I'll be lucky if I can even hang on until the final table."

"Skyler, you sell yourself too short." Clinton reaches his large, rough hand across the console and squeezes my knee. "You're good at this. *Really* fucking good. You don't enter larger tournaments because you get in the way of yourself." He lifts his hand to tap the side of my head. "It's all up here. You psych yourself out."

"But this isn't just a tournament. It'll be on television. People will be watching. People have been practicing all year for this."

Clinton smiles. "Well, then I guess you better not get used to no one knowing your name because after you win this thing, everyone will."

I have no idea why, but my eyes fill with water that I don't blink away. I don't want the tears. I just let them sit there, blurring my vision a bit as I glance at Clinton. "You really think I can do this?"

"I know you can." I let out a large breath and he continues. "In fact, when we get back to campus, we're going straight to my room and signing you up."

"Maybe I should sleep on it."

Clinton shakes his head. "No chance. We're signing you up and then we're booking our flights."

"Our?"

He nods. "Yep. Our. I'm going to be there the first time the poker world wakes up and realizes who Skyler Fucking Thorne is."

At that, I laugh and blink, granting my tears access to roll down my cheeks in two symmetrical rivers. After a few moments of silence, my heart surges and I reach across to grab his hand. "Thank you."

He just squeezes it in response and then reaches forward, raising the volume on the radio. We goof around, sing, and joke about absolutely nothing that makes sense the rest of the way home.

And I silently thank whatever God is listening for sending me Clinton Pennington.

Jess

AH, I LOVE BREAKFAST IN BED.

Or should I say, Jarrett loves breakfast in bed. I just love serving it.

"Oh, fuck," I moan, arching my back and grinding my pelvis against his god-like tongue. "Right there. Yes." I drag out the word, my breaths ragged and intense.

Jarrett just smiles against my tender flesh and continues moving his magical fingers inside me, hitting the spot I need him to touch most. The rough stubble on his face provides just enough friction to drive me mad, and combined with his skilled alternating motions somewhere between sucking and licking, I'm ready to combust any second.

"Come here," I pant, grabbing at the bare skin of his shoulders to coax him up to me. I'm ready for him to be inside me. I need it. Now.

"You come first."

"I want you to fuck me."

He moves his fingers faster and sucks my clit, causing me to cry out his name. "And I will. But first, you're going to come just like this."

Realizing there's no use in arguing, I relax against the sheets and move my hands to cover his gripping my hips. He squeezes harder, his tongue flicking up some sort of magical combination I'm pretty sure they don't even teach at Hogwarts before he sends me flying into ecstasy.

I ride out the orgasm, bucking my hips up to meet his mouth with each wave until I'm spent. When I finish, Jarrett kisses and bites his way up every inch of my body until he meets my mouth, letting me taste myself on his tongue. "You'd do well to listen to me and not argue when I'm trying to pleasure you."

"Oh shut up and fuck me," I moan. He's all too happy to oblige. Flipping me over and pressing my face into his soft goose down comforter, he takes all of six seconds to fill me from behind. My entire body is flat against the bed and my legs are still squeezed tight together as he straddles my ass and pounds into me hard. In this position, I swear I feel him all the way up to my ribcage.

He doesn't come in this position though.

Or the next one. Or the next one after that. No, Jarrett takes his time fucking me all morning, switching positions when I know he's close just so he can ride out another ten minutes. When we're both slick with sweat, our legs aching, our mounting climaxes ridiculously uncomfortable

– that's when he lets me come again and releases with me.

"Goddamn, Jess," he whispers, dropping his forehead against mine. I wait for him to continue, to say something else, but apparently those two words are all he needed to convey what he meant – just my name and the most offensive curse word in the English language.

Oddly, I'm flattered.

He removes himself gently, kissing my lips once more before peeling off the condom and retreating to the bathroom. For a moment I just watch his tight ass waltz away, trailing my eyes along the lines of the tattoos covering both his arms. He rubs his hand over his bald head and half closes the door, blocking my view. Sighing, I spread out in the sheets and flex my muscles, wincing as they ache in protest. Jarrett chuckles from the doorframe a moment later.

"You need a banana and some water."

I quirk my brow at the phallic fruit reference, but decide not to comment on it. "I'm thinking more along the lines of bacon and a mimosa."

"You have class in a half hour."

I shrug. "And? I'll sober up before our test tonight, professor. Promise." I wink and he shakes his head. It's the week after Thanksgiving and already finals have kicked in. Dr. Maynard decided to give us our last test tonight before finals week officially starts next week so we don't feel overwhelmed. It doesn't matter, though. We're college kids – we wait until the last minute and then overdose on Adderall and Red Bull until we get the job done. It's what we do.

"So," Jarrett muses, taking a seat at the edge of the bed and pulling my left foot into his hand. When he gently starts massaging it, I lean my head back and moan. "Are we going to talk about what this is."

"What *what* is?" I ask, my head still against the pillow, eyes closed.

"Don't be naïve," he warns. "After tonight, I won't be your professor's GA anymore."

I lean up on my elbows, but don't pull my foot from his hands. "Are you trying to be my boyfriend, Jarrett Locke?"

"I'm not necessarily trying to title it like that, no."

I frown, but not really because I'm disappointed – more because I'm confused. I mean, I'm not looking for anything serious, either. But then again, what else is there?

Oh. Right.

"So, fuck buddies, then?"

"I'm not necessarily trying to title it like that, either."

I huff, yanking my foot back this time. "So then what exactly *are* you trying to say?"

He shrugs. "I'm just saying I don't want to fuck anyone else. And I don't want *you* to fuck anyone else."

"So, like I said…"

"But I also want to hang out with you."

"But we can't be seen in public because you're a GA for next semester, too – even if I won't be in the class again."

He nods, but for once, he looks sheepish, his normally lusting eyes taking on a childish glow.

I consider it for all of two seconds before abruptly moving from the bed and pulling on my clothes. "Yeah, I don't know about that."

"What don't you know about? What's there to question?" I just give him a pointed look, my long blonde locks falling in my face a bit as I do. My hair is usually shiny and radiant, but since I've been in his bed for two straight days, it's taken on a greasy appearance instead. Hastily, I tie it in a messy bun and let it sit on my head.

"What if I just see you when I see you?"

Jarrett stands, towering over me as he moves his hands to my waist and pulls me into him. "We've already established that no one on that campus can fuck you into oblivion like I can. So what are you going to do? Buy a new vibrator? Name it after me and pretend it's half as good?"

I scoff. "Cocky bastard." I try to peel myself away from him but his grip remains firm.

"You and I both know when I'm being cocky and this is not one of those times." He pauses, his intense dark eyes searching mine. "I'm being serious. And honest. You should try it."

"I don't want this to be complicated."

"Me either."

Sighing, I pull my tank top over my head but it stops where his hands are still firmly planted. Jarrett does make a good point. I've never met a man who can give me pleasure the way he does. And I know when I leave here all I'm going to think about is the next time I can come back.

So I cave.

"Okay." Jarrett smirks but I poke my finger hard into his chest. "But if shit gets complicated or dramatic, we end it. I'm serious."

"Deal."

I eye him cautiously. "Okay."

"Okay."

AFTER MY TEST in Scope and Methods, I meet the girls at Ralph's for drinks. Finals week is about to really kick in and we know we won't see each other much until the celebratory parties next weekend. They're all chatting animatedly, but I can't stop staring at Ashlei and Bo. They're sitting right next to each other, laughing and talking to us like nothing happened at semi-formal.

And it's really irking me.

I never called them out on their shit. In fact, I haven't talked to either of them since semi, but they haven't questioned it because it was Thanksgiving and now we're all in finals mode. Ashlei is always sneaking off anyway. Now, anytime she disappears when Bo isn't around, I can't help but wonder if that's where she's going.

But, then again, staring at them now, I can't help but wonder if maybe it was just a drunken kiss. Hell, I've kissed a few girls in my drunken state of shenanigans – it's not like it doesn't happen. Still... something feels off.

"Ready to be roomies next semester, Cassie?" Bo asks, cheersing our little red head from across the table. I have to admit, I was a little skeptical about Cassie when I first met her. I wasn't sure how she'd fit in with us. I'm not that close with her yet, but she has easily melded into our group and I love the color she brings to it.

"I'm ready to be out of the hellish situation I'm in right now, that's for sure," she says, clinking Bo's glass before taking a sip. "Paris will be in the Zeta house next semester, too. I guess it was only a matter of time."

Ashlei shakes her head. "I have plenty of girlfriends in other sororities. If Paris ended your friendship, it's because that was her choice." I kind of blanch at the term girlfriends, wondering if there's more to that than she lets on, but I decide not to press it.

"I'm going to miss her," Cassie mumbles, trailing the condensation on her glass.

Skyler gently pats her back. "And there's nothing wrong with that."

"Except that you're not allowed to miss her anymore because you're clearly in better company now," Erin adds, winking at her Grand Little.

"I'm more curious about how your night went after semi-formal," I add. We made jokes about how we both went with frat presidents that night. The difference is I left without mine. She didn't.

Cassie's cheeks blush a furious shade of red that almost competes with her hair and she immediately sucks down half her drink. "It was fine."

My eyes scan the other girls and they're all looking around the table, too, before we burst into a fit of laughter. Cassie covers her face with her hands and tosses a napkin in my direction.

"You guys are the worst."

"Hey," I say, throwing my hands up. "Ain't no shame in getting some penis action. Clearly I'm not going to judge."

Everyone laughs harder at that before the topic of conversation changes to Erin and her application for Recruitment Chair. It's a ballsy move, especially since there are at least three other senior girls going for the same position. They've been waiting over three years to get their shot at that chair, but something tells me it's going to go to Erin anyway. She always has everything under control and the entire chapter knows that no one can run recruitment and bring us a better pledge class next fall than she can.

"So, since we're not going to be together for New Year's Eve, I want to hear everyone's resolutions right now," Erin says and we all groan in unison. She's all about the sharing/sisterhood shit and even though we all secretly love it, too, we pretend like it's annoying. Mostly because it's fun to tease Erin.

She gives us all a pointed look, but lifts her glass. "Oh, stop. Little, you go first."

Skyler blows out a long breath before lifting her glass to join Erin's. "I resolve to stop being afraid of what might happen if I take risks. Starting with this tournament." We all smile at that, even if we don't fully understand it. I certainly have no interest in poker or her obsession with it, but I can tell from how she's been talking that this Atlantic City tournament is a big deal. So, obviously, I'm going to support her.

Cassie raises her cup next. "I'm going to ace my classes and get a head start on my pre-med program." Ashlei and I give her pointed looks and she concedes. "Okay fine, I'll have a little more fun, too."

It's not quite good enough for me, but again, I let it go. Little Miss Innocent can stay our little angel for a while longer.

Bo toasts to new beginnings and Ashlei ditto's her as they lift their glasses in unison. The soft and knowing look they exchange isn't lost on me and I frown, thrusting my drink up next. "Well, other than changing my major because clearly political science is not for me, I resolve to be honest. I just think honesty is an important virtue and I'm making it a priority."

Nearly everyone at the table seems uncomfortable at my toast, but I hold my glass high along with my head and smile.

"I resolve to bring us the best pledge class yet when I'm elected Recruitment Chair," Erin finishes us off. None of us even comment on the fact that she didn't say *if*. We all know she'll get the job.

We clink our glasses together and say "Happy New Year" in unison before throwing back the liquid. Bo hugs me, which is surprising, and asks me to study for finals with her this weekend. I agree, because I really do need to get closer to her – especially if I expect her to grow our family tree next year. I consider telling them about my recent romps with Jarrett and what we agreed to at his apartment this morning, but as I open my mouth I think better of it.

For once, I'm going to keep my little private affair to myself.

"Drink up, ladies," Skyler says, signaling for the bartender to return to us. "We survived another semester at Palm South University."

Scanning the faces of my beautiful sisters, I can't help but wonder how many secrets survived right along with us.

Adam

THIS HAS TO BE A JOKE.

That's all I can think as I stare at Clay. His blue eyes are hard, like he's pissed the words are coming from his mouth just as much as I'm surprised by them. Running his hands back through his dirty blonde hair, he repeats them again, but I still don't understand.

So this time, I say it out loud.

"This has to be a joke."

Clay purses his lips, but then takes a deep breath and crosses his arms hard over his chest. "It's not. Tommy is transferring and that leaves Social Chair open. Since you practically did his job this semester anyway, it only makes sense that you step into the position officially." He shifts and I can tell he hates admitting any of this.

"Is this some sort of peace offering?"

"In a way, I guess," he admits. "But honestly, I still think you're a little punk who has no respect for older brothers. That aside, you did get us recognized a lot this semester. You're the best brother for the job. That's a fact I can't ignore as president."

PALM SOUTH UNIVERSITY 1

If I weren't focusing so hard on clamping my jaw shut, my mouth would be hanging wide open. Is this really Clay right now? Where's the colossal asshat I'm so used to dealing with?

"So, are you in?"

Shaking my thoughts, I nod. "Yeah. Of course. I, uh, thank you. Thanks for this." I sound like an idiot, but this is the most cordial conversation I've ever had with Clay. It's fucking weird.

Clay nods and extends his hand to me. We shake firmly and then walk side by side back into our fraternity house. For once, it's quiet – mostly because our Academic Chair has deemed the house a study zone for finals.

Before I can stop myself, I clear my throat and ask Clay the question that's been burning in the back of my mind for weeks now. "So, how is Cassie?"

Clay smirks, and it's like the douchebag I've always known emerged out of him to overpower the professional stand-in. "Oh, she's *amazing*." He cocks a brow in a sideways glance at me in a way that suggests he means that in every sense of the word. "Something about the little innocent ones, isn't there? It's almost like you get to play the role of teacher."

I grind my teeth together. "Clay, don't be a fucking dick. She deserves your respect and you know it."

"Oh, of course," he agrees. "And she got it. All night long after semi-formal." His slimy grin grows wider and I shove him hard against his chest. He stumbles back, his legs hitting the arm of our couch and he just falls down to sit in it, laughing hysterically. I consider rushing him again but he stands, wiping the corners of his eyes. "Ah, man, next semester's going to be fun." He claps me hard on the back. "Welcome to the Executive Board, Brooks."

With that, he turns and practically struts down the hall to the President's Room, still chuckling to himself. I growl, frustrated, and make my way into the kitchen to grab a beer. Cracking back the top and sucking down half of the can, I let the icy liquid cool my temper and inhale a deep breath. When my phone pings in and I see a text from Skyler, I smile.

- I need a study break. Come to your window. ;) -

I throw back the rest of my beer and jog down the hall to my room, locking the door behind me. When I yank down on the string to lift my blinds, Skyler's aqua eyes meet mine. She smiles seductively and bites her lip and I just shake my head, lifting the window and immediately covering her mouth with mine.

"What happened to not seeing each other until after finals?"

"I lied," she says simply, breaking from my kiss long enough to crawl through the window. She's dressed casually in a tiny pair of dark jean shorts and a light purple Kappa Kappa Beta tank top. It was freezing just a couple of weeks ago but, in typical Florida fashion, it feels almost like summer again today.

I'm about to offer Skyler a drink when she presses her lips to mine again and slides her hand down to grip me through my basketball shorts, effectively silencing my words. My cock immediately responds to her touch and I back her up to my bed, pulling her down into the sheets. She bites my neck and I hiss through the slight shock of pain as her long brown hair falls all around us.

Flipping her head back and still straddling me, Skyler smiles down at me with hooded eyes as she grinds her hips against mine.

"You look a little stressed," she whispers, slowly winding. "Let me help."

Maneuvering herself to sit between my legs, she fists my shorts and boxers together in her hands and pulls them down over my thighs. I kick them the rest of the way off and she grips my cock firmly, stroking from the tip down to the bottom of my shaft and back. I bite my lip and let my eyes roll back at the feel of her hands, groaning.

"Hey," she whispers and I open my eyes just enough to peer down at her. Still grinning, she twists her long locks up and piles them in a mess on top of her head. "I forgot a hair tie." She grabs my hand and moves it to replace where hers was holding her hair up. "Keep it out of my way."

With that she licks her lips, her blue eyes dazzling in the low light of the afternoon sun streaming in through my window, and then her mouth is on me.

Holy. Mother. Fucking. Fuck.

Skyler swirls her tongue around my tip before pressing her lips firmly against my skin and pushing lower. She takes me in completely with a slight gag and I curse under my breath, fisting her hair tightly. When she moans, I feel the vibrations through her throat and with her slick, hot mouth it's a deadly combination.

She alternates teasing my head with deep throating, every move pushing me closer to climax. Every time I get close, though, she removes her mouth and flattens her tongue, running it from the base to the tip and back down with just enough pressure to tease me but take away the mounting pressure. She's good – *so* fucking good. I've had plenty of blow jobs over the years but nothing could compare to how she's making me feel right now.

When she twists her hands over my shaft to fill the space her mouth isn't covering and works them in combination, I stop breathing and the fiery numbness starts to consume me.

"Fuck, Skyler," I growl. "I'm coming."

I try to pull out of her mouth to finish but she doesn't budge, digging her nails into my thighs in protest. When her devilish eyes gaze up into mine through her lashes while her mouth is still wrapped around me, the visual is too much and I throw my head back against the bed and explode. She doesn't stop working as I bust inside her mouth, my entire body consumed with the intense pleasure she's inflicting. I still as I finish, my body falling limp, and Skyler just pulls back, swallows, and smiles.

Goddamn.

She crawls back up to lay on my chest and I numbly run my fingers through her hair. When I catch my breath and try to roll her over to repay the favor, she stops me, wrapping her arms around me and snuggling back into my chest.

"Today was for you."

"What?" I ask, leaning up slightly. She peers up at me and smiles contently.

"I wanted to please my boyfriend. What's so surprising about that?" She's still smiling but when she sees my face, she realizes what she said and her smile drops. I wait for her to recant, but she doesn't.

"Boyfriend?"

She swallows, but again, doesn't take it back.

I consider it for a moment, wondering if either of us is ready to be in any kind of steady relationship. We're about to break for Christmas and next semester we'll both be busy, as usual. Then again, I don't have any interest in fucking around with any other girls, and Skyler doesn't seem like the overbearing type of girlfriend. She's beautiful, funny, and talented – *in many ways*. What's holding me back?

"Well, I guess I'll allow it. As long as I can pay you back next time."

Skyler looks visibly relieved and she smiles again, leaning in to kiss me. "Looking forward to it."

She rests on my chest again and I continue gently trailing my fingers over her shoulder and up into her hair. "Clay made me Social Chair."

"Yeah?" Skyler asks lazily, her eyes closed. "Not surprising to me. You practically do it all already, right?"

I nod. "Yeah. I guess now it's just titled and official."

She smiles and squeezes me tighter. "I've never slept with a man of such power."

I scoff. "What, Omega Chi presidents don't count?"

Skyler nails me hard in the stomach and I double over but laugh and pull her into me. She squeals and fakes like she's trying to get away before giving up.

"You're an ass."

"And you have a nice ass. Look! We're perfect together."

She rolls her eyes but settles back into my chest with a smile. "I'm so tired," she says, yawning. "Can I nap here for a while? It's so much quieter than our house."

I kiss her forehead in response and in less than a minute, her breathing steadies out and I know she's asleep.

I try to think of the last time I had a girlfriend. I was hooking up with several girls last year, and I think Jazmine might have put a title on us at one point – though I didn't really abide by said title. Still, Skyler doesn't strike me as the type of girl to get hung up on titles. I wonder if it almost slipped as an accident but she was just afraid to take it back and hurt my feelings. Regardless, I like her – a lot – and now at least I have some reassurance that no other guys will be touching her the way I do. Relaxing against Skyler, I let my exhaustion from the day take me under and decide not to overthink it.

But just before I drift off, my mind wanders to a shy redhead with soft green eyes.

Bear

I'M A LITTLE NERVOUS as I stride into the Kappa Kappa Beta house and back to their chapter room where all the girls are seated. It's the last chapter of the year and election night, which means they've already had a long meeting and are probably dying to get out of the room. Skyler just texted me less than ten minutes ago to let me know Erin was elected Recruitment Chair. When I find Erin at the front of the room, she looks insanely happy – maybe more so than I've ever seen, but her face falls when she sees me.

I still can't fucking believe I hooked up with Erin Xander. Even more hilarious, she thought *I* would go around telling people. Is she crazy? There's a reason that chick is known around Greek world as Ex. The girl has gone through boyfriends like designer shoes the past three years. No way am I in any way interested in being added to that list – especially since she has the reputation to not know how to let shit go.

Yeah, fuck all that.

I just smile at her briefly to show her she doesn't need to worry before I turn with my brothers to face the rest of the room.

"Good evening, beautiful ladies of KKB. The brothers of Omega Chi Beta wish you all a fun and safe winter break and look forward to next semester. We brought you all chocolate to celebrate the end of finals," I add with a smile. The girls all cheer and clap and the guys laugh. Girls fucking love chocolate.

"I also wanted to take a minute to share something else with you ladies," I say, swallowing back the nerves. I have no idea why I even have them. "I'm not good with words, so I won't make this too long, but some of you may have noticed that Skyler Thorne is a pretty amazing girl." All the sisters smile and turn to stare at Skyler, who's seated near the back. She just smiles at me and suddenly I'm not the least bit nervous anymore. "She and I met last year during Spring Break and we've become closer every day since then. I can't think of anyone else in the world who I care about more than I do her. There are some people who help you through tough times, but then there are some who help you hold on when you think you have nothing else left to grip. Skyler, you are the best friend I have ever had and I could never thank you enough for always being there for me." Even from across the room, I see her eyes gloss over. I shake my head. "Okay, fuck this sappy shit." The room bursts into laughter and I make my way up the makeshift aisle between where the chairs are set and hold out a bouquet of flowers to Skyler. "Sky, I want to officially ask you to be my Little Sister."

The room explodes with a deafening cheer and Skyler laughs, eyes still laminated in a film of unshed tears. She nods and jumps up to throw her tiny arms around my thick neck. I squeeze her in return and she takes the flowers, slugging me on the arm and wiping at her face. "Damn you for making me all emotional."

I throw her a wink and toss my arm around her shoulder before addressing the rest of the room again. "Now all of you go change and get your cute asses down to the O Chi house. Our alumni told us not to party for the rest of the semester and technically finals are over. So, fuck it! Let's rage!"

The cheers ring out even louder and Skyler throws her fist into the air. Quickly, she plants a kiss on my cheek and then jogs off to join her sisters as they filter out of the room. My brothers clap me on the back and we exit the house, joking and singing our obnoxious fraternity drinking songs the entire way back to the house. My Little, Josh, starts the party as soon as we make it back inside, blasting the stereo and breaking out our liquor bottle stash while some of the younger brothers call about getting last minute kegs. Even on short notice, there's no party better than an Omega Chi party.

I haven't heard a single word from anyone other than my younger brother since I gave my mom that check. And, for once, I'm actually happy about it. I feel like a weight has been lifted and Skyler has made me realize that I have a new family here at Palm South. I'm spending Christmas break with her and her family so we can prep her for the big tournament in Atlantic City and I can't imagine a better way to end the semester. It's been a rough and crazy ride, but right now I feel at peace.

And I am beyond ready to rage.

Cassie

I MADE IT THROUGH my first semester at Palm South University.

Red Solo cup in hand, I snake my way in-between other Greek students stuffed into the Omega Chi house and make my way back over to Skyler and Jess. Now that finals are over and all that's left to do is celebrate, everyone is in a better mood. Jess has been distant and bitchy lately, but she has a huge smile plastered on her face tonight. Ashlei, Bo, and Erin are playing flip cup against Clinton and two of his brothers across the room. Skyler looks relaxed, and for once I don't see the impending tournament weighing on her. It's like we're all filled with a sense of accomplishment and joy tonight.

Nothing can bring us down.

I'm well on my way to a nice buzz when Skyler and Adam challenge me and Jess to a game of beer pong. We claim one of the empty tables and Adam and I grab beer while Jess and Skyler set up the water cups. We haven't talked since the night of semi-formal, and I feel an awkward tension set in between us as we reach the kegs.

"I heard you're going to be the new Social Chair," I say after filling the third cup. I move it to rest on a small table with the others and grab the next.

Adam smiles. "I'm sorry, Cassie."

"For moving into a leadership position?"

He chuckles and it does something to my stomach that makes me falter the keg nozzle a bit. "No, for being a douche to you. I know you're too nice to call me out on my shit, but I'm not too proud to admit I was wrong. I shouldn't have been in your business that night."

My cheeks burn and I shrug, topping off the last cup. "It's whatever. I haven't even thought about it. Really," I lie with a forced smile. We both balance our cups, gripping them by the lips three in each hand as we make our way back to the table.

"Well, good. I've missed my friend. Let's get breakfast tomorrow morning before everyone heads out."

His dark hair has grown out over the semester and as it falls into his eyes a bit, I can't help the grin that curls on my lips. "Okay."

Adam and Skyler win the first game but Jess and I win the second. I learn that the more intoxicated I get, the easier it seems to be to land that little white pong ball in the cups across the table. We're halfway through the tie-breaker game when I spot Clay sitting on the couch behind where Adam is standing.

And Paris is sitting on his lap.

Handing my ball to Jess without taking my eyes off them, I cross to where they sit and nervously fold my hands together. They don't seem to notice as Clay's hand moves further up where it's resting on Paris' bare thigh. "Hey, Clay."

He's mid-laughter, his mouth close to Paris' neck when I interrupt. They both turn in unison to face me and Paris tucks a long strand of her crimson hair behind her ear, smiling sweetly at me though I feel her intentions are laced with poison. We barely talk anymore, but she knows I've been with Clay since Halloween, which is why this scenario doesn't make any sense to me.

"Oh, hey Cass. What's up?"

I shift. "Uh, what are you doing?" God, I suck at this. How do I confront him? He never said we were boyfriend and girlfriend but still, there were things said. There were things... done.

"Actually, Paris was just telling me that you two are roomies." He turns back to her with a devilish smirk. "My imagination is running wild with that thought."

Paris giggles, and it's as if it breaks the fragile band that was holding me together. "What the hell is wrong with you?" I snap.

Clay's smile falls as he looks back up at me and I realize I called attention to us, which was definitely not what I intended. Clay doesn't seem fazed in the least. "Oh, Cassie," he says, speaking to me like a child. "You didn't think that because we hooked up we were…" he trails off, his hand covering his mouth a bit as he turns to face Paris momentarily before my eyes again. "Oh shit. You did, didn't you?"

"That's so adorable," Paris says, still smiling. I know I'm blushing furiously as I snap my attention to her and plead with my eyes for my best friend to emerge. Where is she? Where's the girl who was practically my sister just four short months ago? Have I lost her completely?

When she just smiles wider, revealing her perfect white teeth, I know I've found my answer.

I want to yell. I want to scream. I want to make them both feel small and insignificant but for some reason, tears prick the corners of my eyes instead. I whip around and storm toward the door. Adam tries to grab my arm and calls out for me but I shake him loose. When I push through the door out onto Greek row, Skyler follows closely behind me. I don't turn around as I all but sprint to the KKB house, but Skyler still trails me. When I finally make it, I punch in our door code and immediately fall onto the couch, letting the tears fall.

I swipe at them furiously, pissed that I'm letting those two assholes affect me this way, but the rivers of betrayal just keep streaming down my cheeks. Skyler doesn't speak a word when she enters through the door, but she sinks down next to me and pulls my head onto her shoulder. It's such a simple and comforting move, but for some reason it breaks me more and I sob harder.

"Shh," she coos, rubbing my back softly. "It's okay. Clay's a dick, Little Nug. He doesn't deserve your tears."

And I know that, but there's so much more to it than Skyler could understand. She continues consoling me, attempting to make me laugh by pointing out oddities in Paris' appearance and making fun of Clay's "Ken Smile". Eventually, I do stop crying, and I pull back from her embrace.

"Thanks, Big. You should get back," I say, nodding toward the direction of the O Chi house. "It's the last party of the semester. Don't miss it on my account."

"You don't want to come back? Prove to everyone that you couldn't care less about those two twat-lickers?"

I force a small smile, but it falls too quickly. "I just want to be alone. Can I sleep in your room for a while?"

"Of course," she says, pulling me in for another long hug.

After Skyler leaves, I crawl into her bed and curl up in the covers, facing the wall. I close my eyes, steady out my breathing, and clear my head, but still, sleep doesn't come. Instead, I feel an overwhelming emotion take hold that I've never experienced in my eighteen years of life. It's something I hoped I never would have to feel, especially not this intensely. But, here it is, washing through me and leaving a sticky residue behind.

Regret.

I WAKE LATER, my eyes puffy and my cheeks still hot as I lean up and check the clock on Jess' side of the room. She's absent and Skyler is in her bed. It's just after five in the morning.

Quietly, I slip out of Skyler's soft lavender sheets and tiptoe out of the room. After slipping on my Keds, I start walking down Greek Row. It's pitch black outside and cool, but there's a hint of dawn on the horizon and I let it comfort me as my feet numbly carry me to the Alpha Sigma house. When I'm finally standing outside his window, my stomach flips, but I softly rap on it with my knuckles anyway. It only takes a minute for two chocolate eyes to peer out at me through the blinds.

When the blinds shoot up, Adam stands in their place in nothing but green and blue plaid boxer shorts. His hair is disheveled, his eyes squinted from sleep, and his brows slightly furrowed as he takes me in. He lifts the window and holds out his hand, helping me climb inside. I kick off my shoes and crawl into his bed first, pulling the covers up and over my shoulders and facing the wall just like I did in Skyler's room. His sheets smell like him, a mixture of mint and his Burberry cologne, and I inhale deep as he slides in the sheets behind me.

Hesitantly, he snakes his arm under mine and pulls me into him, aligning his body with mine. Even though I can feel every muscle of his abdomen pressed against my back, it's still a friendly gesture, and I don't feel uncomfortable or like we're doing anything wrong. He holds me like a friend who knows he may be the only person who can keep my cracking pieces from splitting completely right now.

"You were right," I whisper.

He sighs and I feel the air softly blow the back of my neck. He holds me tighter around my middle and buries his head into my back, his lips just barely touching the skin left exposed from my tank top.

"I wish I wasn't."

For a moment he just holds me, neither of us saying anything else. I know I'm not falling asleep anytime soon and I feel like Adam isn't either, but we don't make any moves to get up and do anything else. When he does speak again, his voice is softer than before.

"Skyler and I made things official."

I swallow and he waits for me to respond, but I'm not sure how to. I know they're together. They've been together for a while now. Yet somehow, hearing that they're official hits me hard in the gut and I curl up into myself tighter. Adam doesn't release his grip on me though, which comforts and confuses me both.

I could comment on what he said, but what do I really say at this point? I'm happy for them, Adam knows that. He knows I would never say otherwise. At the same time, I feel like he's waiting for me to say the words I haven't even quite formed on my own yet.

In the end, I don't speak again. I just nod and smile, which Adam takes for what it's worth. His thumb lazily rubs against my lower stomach and I close my eyes tight, one lone tear escaping and falling to his pillow silently and without him noticing. Even though Skyler comforted me earlier, for some reason having Adam hold me makes me truly feel like everything will be okay. Even so, there's still something neither of them know that is the reason for most of my tears tonight.

I'm upset that Paris is no longer my best friend. I'm confused about my feelings for Adam. I'm hurt that Clay spoke words to me he didn't mean before laying me down in his room just a few feet down the hall from where I lie in Adam's right now. But, more than that, I regret that I didn't listen to Adam that night when he warned me. I hate myself for giving something so precious to someone who feels absolutely nothing for me. Clay wasn't just the first guy at Palm South I've had sex with.

He was the first.

Period.

Ashlei

"I'M GOING TO MISS YOU GIRLS!" Erin pulls us each in for a hug, squeezing us a little too tightly.

"Oh yeah, I'm sure you'll be thinking of us every minute while you romp around Europe over break," Jess says sarcastically.

"Hush, you. I'm serious. Promise me you'll all call."

"We will," Skyler assures, throwing one arm around Cassie's shoulders. Cassie's eyes are dark, her face long. I don't talk to her much – hell, I guess I haven't really been around enough this semester to form much of a relationship with anyone – but even I can tell she's not okay right now. Hopefully winter break in Phoenix will help her get back on track.

Erin's town car pulls up just as she hoists her bag up onto her shoulder. She offers one last wave before climbing inside. Jess leaves next, blowing us all a kiss and then flipping us off as she climbs into her Beamer. Clinton pulls up not too long after in a cab and Cassie and Skyler climb in. They're hitting the airport for Cassie to catch her flight and Skyler to grab a rental car for the trip home. Bo and I wish her luck at the tournament and then it's just us.

"I'm going to miss you," I say honestly, tucking my pinkie into her front jean pocket. I consider asking her to go back in the house with me to properly say goodbye, but her parents will be here any minute.

"I know. It's only a few weeks, though."

She's so damn beautiful. Her dark hair is pin straight and shaping the thin features of her face as her almond eyes appraise me. It's like she's trying to figure me out. Or maybe, how she feels when she's with me.

Lord knows it's not an easy feeling to digest.

Life has been a whirl since semi-formal. We took what we have – whatever that is – to the next level, for sure. Yet, at the same time, we still haven't really talked about what that means. Still, staring at her now, beautiful smile wide on her face, I don't really care what we are – as long as we're something.

"Uh, Lei?" she asks suddenly, her face falling. "Is that…"

I turn to where her eyes are focused and my heart stops before hammering in my chest. Kya is standing on the other side of our front yard, leaning against her black Jeep. She's dyed her hair a bright pink and streaked it with bleach blonde since the last time I've seen her. Even leaned up against her car, she's still as tall as Hayden and intimidating as hell. Her green eyes are fierce, yet turned down as she waits for me.

"Hang on," I murmur to Bo before crossing the yard. When I make it to Kya, she stands straighter, only making me feel worse.

"Sorry to interrupt your goodbyes," she says, casting a glance at Bo before landing her eyes back on mine.

"What do you want, Kya? There's no practice today."

She sighs. "You still owe me, Ashlei."

"What?" I blanch, then shake my head. "No, I paid you. I gave you the ten thousand." After semi-formal, I swallowed my pride and asked my parents for the cash to pay Kya and be done with the whole situation. I told them it was for a study abroad program this summer and they gave it without question. I felt awful lying to them and I'll have to figure out what the hell to do about my actual summer situation later, but for the time being, my problems were solved.

So what the hell is Kya talking about?

"Hayden stole a kilo from me, Ashlei," she says with a sigh. "My supplier threatened him with his life if he didn't pay. He lied about what happened and threw your name in the mix." I stiffen at her words, but she just continues. "He skipped town. It's on you now."

"What? But you told them it wasn't true, right?"

She nods. "I did, but it doesn't matter, Ashlei. You can't reason with these guys. You were a part of this and the ten thousand you paid barely covers any of what was stolen."

"Jesus," I murmur, pressing my clammy hand to my forehead. "A fucking kilo? What did he do with it?"

Kya shrugs. "I don't know. He probably snorted some of it himself and sold the rest or used it to party. You know Hayden."

But that's the thing. I thought I knew him, but clearly, I was wrong.

"Kya, we have to go talk to this guy you owe. I only did the shit three times and I've already paid for that plus some. We can talk him off of this."

She shifts. "I don't need to talk to him, Ashlei. He doesn't blame me, not since Hayden told him what happened."

"But Hayden lied!"

"I know," she says, holding up her hands to calm me. "I'm sorry, Ashlei. You have to pay them the rest. Just call your parents and ask for more."

"I can't do that, Kya. They're not a fucking ATM."

She looks at me like she doubts that, but then frowns. "There's only one other option for you to pay them and trust me, you don't want to take plan B. Just call your parents. Make up another lie."

"I'm not paying them. Fuck this. I didn't do shit."

"Ashlei, please," she begs. "You have to listen to me. They will come after you." Her voice grows quiet. "They'll find ways to make you pay." Her eyes shift to Bo and I swallow.

"How much more?"

"Thirty thousand."

I blanch. That's three times what I've already paid.

"There's no way my parents will just hand that over." I pinch the bridge of my nose and shake my head. "What's my other option?"

Kya cocks her head in warning but when she sees I'm serious, she sighs. "My supplier's name is Xavier Rojas. He owns a high-end club downtown. He said," she pauses, considering her words carefully. "He told me if you couldn't get the money, he would let you work to pay it off."

"Really?" I ask excitedly. "Well, that's no problem. I can work. What does he need? Bartenders and stuff?"

She swallows, and I take a moment to think about what else he could mean.

Then my stomach drops.

"He wants me to dance, doesn't he?"

She nods.

"Oh my God," I whisper, shaking my head. Pole dancing is an art to me – a sport, a release, a personal challenge. I would never dance for money. I would never *strip* for money. "I can't. I *won't* do that."

"What other choice do you have?" Kya asks, her eyes soft and sad. I hate her for telling me this, but I know she doesn't mean to hurt me. It's Hayden who fucked me over. It's him I should hate, and he's not even in the state – hell, he might not even be in the country. Kya is just covering her own ass, and if what she says about Xavier is true, can I really blame her for not shifting his focus back to her, even if she doesn't want to see me hurt?

Then again, maybe she couldn't give two shits what happens to me. We're not friends. We dance together, sure – but at the end of the day, the troupe isn't a family. It's not a sisterhood.

It's not Kappa Kappa Beta.

There's no way my parents will fork over that amount of cash, not unless I tell them what happened, which I definitely can't do. I could ask the girls, but that would involve telling them about my life outside of Palm South – another option I can't consider. I can't lose KKB. I can't lose my sisters.

Casting a sideways glance at Bo, I scan her face as she nonverbally asks me what's going on. How did I end up here? How did I land myself in this shithole? And what the hell do I do now? My palms sweat as I consider my options. I rack my brain for a way out, for a way to make this nightmare disappear, but I come up short.

"Well?" Kya interrupts my thoughts and I turn to face her again. My head is spinning, my mouth is dry, my heart is thundering against my rib cage and threatening to knock me down to the cold earth. When she speaks the next words, I almost can't hear them through the ringing in my ears.

"What are you going to do?"

Join the Palm South University Discussion Group on Facebook to keep up to date on future seasons!

Acknowledgements

I'm going to do my best to make these acknowledgements short and sweet like the PSU episodes. We'll see how that actually turns out. I'd like to first thank my fan group, #KandisChasers, for this one. It's because of you that this serial is even happening. You read Black Number Four and begged for more of your favorite characters. Thank you for making me see I wasn't quite ready to leave PSU, either. I love y'all. Oh and Shawna, I made Hayden eat a wiener for you. You're welcome.

As always, thank you to my husband, Ryan, for always supporting my writing endeavors. It's not easy being married to a writer and I truly appreciate all the sacrifices you make for my dream. I love you! Mom, thanks for continuing to love and support me, even with the miles between us. I always know I have you on my team. To "the girls" who these characters are named after – the real Cassie (Graham), Jess (Vogel), Ashlei (Davison), and Erin (Spencer) – thanks for being so damn awesome that I wanted to name characters after you. Our circle of trust is so special to me and I thank God every day that I have y'all. PS Erin – you're not evil yet!

Shout out to the PSU beta readers – Kellee Fabre, Sasha Whittington, Jess Vogel, Ashlei Davison, and Jacquelyn Hansen. When everyone else tapped out on me, you were still there. Your feedback and critique made this series what it is and I truly appreciate your time and attention. Smooches! Betsy Kash, thanks for getting shit done as always and finding time to edit for me even with your crazy schedule. Elaine York, thank you for the beautiful formatting and editing the last two episodes when I was in a time crunch. You both made this little penny shine. Staci Hart. Staci Fucking Hart. Thank you for girl crushing on me just as hard as I girl crush on you. You provided invaluable insight on this serial and also helped me celebrate its little milestones along the way. I can't thank you enough for that. BESOS, BITCH. To you, the reader who read with me each week, discussed your favorite characters, theorized about what would happen, told your friends to join the madness, and so much more – THANK YOU. Thanks for reading indie and for trying new things. I hope you had fun, and don't worry – I won't make you wait too long for next season. And as always, to God Almighty in Heaven. Thank you for the blessings you continue to shower me with. I promise to never take a single one for granted.

About the Author

Kandi Steiner is a bestselling author and whiskey connoisseur living in Tampa, FL. Best known for writing "emotional rollercoaster" stories, she loves bringing flawed characters to life and writing about real, raw romance — in all its forms. No two Kandi Steiner books are the same, and if you're a lover of angsty, emotional, and inspirational reads, she's your gal.

An alumna of the University of Central Florida, Kandi graduated with a double major in Creative Writing and Advertising/PR with a minor in Women's Studies. She started writing back in the 4th grade after reading the first Harry Potter installment. In 6th grade, she wrote and edited her own newspaper and distributed to her classmates. Eventually, the principal caught on and the newspaper was quickly halted, though Kandi tried fighting for her "freedom of press." She took particular interest in writing romance after college, as she has always been a die hard hopeless romantic, and likes to highlight all the challenges of love as well as the triumphs.

When Kandi isn't writing, you can find her reading books of all kinds, talking with her extremely vocal cat, and spending time with her friends and family. She enjoys live music, traveling, anything heavy in carbs, beach days, movie marathons, craft beer and sweet wine — not necessarily in that order.

CONNECT WITH KANDI:
NEWSLETTER: bit.ly/NewsletterKS
FACEBOOK: facebook.com/kandisteiner
FACEBOOK READER GROUP (Kandiland): facebook.com/groups/
kandischasers
INSTAGRAM: Instagram.com/kandisteiner
TWITTER: twitter.com/kandisteiner
PINTEREST: pinterest.com/kandicoffman
WEBSITE: www.kandisteiner.com

Kandi Steiner may be coming to a city near you! Check out her "events" tab to see all the signings she's attending in the near future www.kandisteiner.com/events

More from Kandi Steiner

The What He Doesn't Know Duet
What He Doesn't Know
What He Always Knew

On the Way to You

A Love Letter to Whiskey

Weightless

Revelry

Black Number Four

The Palm South University Series
Rush (Palm South University 1)
Anchor (Palm South University 2)
Pledge (Palm South University 3)
Legacy (Palm South University 4)

The Chaser Series
Tag Chaser
Song Chaser
Straight, No Chaser
Tag Catcher

Made in the USA
San Bernardino, CA
28 May 2020